JENNIFER S. ALDERSON

Death by Fountain

A Christmas Murder in Rome

D1521366

To my American family and friends—I miss you!

Contents

1

Christmas Shopping in The Eternal City

December 17—Piazza Navona, Italy

"Do they have one of those nativity scenes in a larger size? That baby Jesus is way too small." Dotty Thompson's voice crackled through Lana Hansen's telephone speaker, making it difficult to hear her clearly. The wind whipping through the market stalls was not helping matters. As another gust took hold, several of the lighter ornaments flew off of their racks, to the dismay of the many shopkeepers crowding the space.

Lana scanned the cramped stall filled with handcrafted Christmas decorations as she looked for a manger scene that would please Dotty, her boss and the owner of Wanderlust Tours. In addition to decorated glass balls, religious figurines, and miniatures of Rome's most famous icons, this shop also sold a magnificent selection of nativity scenes. Her eyes zoomed in on two planks dedicated to tiny porcelain figurines portraying Joseph, Mary, and the three wise men, as well as cribs made from real twigs and straw, with a baby Jesus resting in each. *Which one would Dotty like the most?* she wondered.

Since arriving in Rome a few hours earlier, Lana and her fellow Wanderlust Tours guide, Randy Wright, had spent most of their time in Piazza Navona's Christmas and Epiphany Market, doing Dotty's holiday shopping. The long, rectangular space was filled with the sounds of shoppers, musicians, happy children, and the twinkly jingle of a wooden-horse merry-go-round. Lights

1

shaped like stars, Christmas trees, and comets topped most of the market stalls. The smell of sugar-coated desserts and hearty bread filled Lana's nostrils.

Luckily, the market was located in one of Rome's most popular tourist spots, considered so thanks to the iconic fountains and buildings that filled the square. In the center of the Piazza Navona rose an Egyptian obelisk, a stone dove with an olive twig in its beak perched on its crown. The gigantic monument rested atop a mass of carved stone, which rose out of an enormous fountain decorated with palm trees, papal symbols, a lion, a serpent, a crocodile, and a dolphin.

Lana knew from her guidebook that it was the Fountain of the Four Rivers by one of Rome's most famous artists, Gian Lorenzo Bernini. Four God-like figures, each representing one of the world's major tributaries, rested on the rocks holding up the obelisk. Staring down at her was the river god Ganges, casually holding an oar as he gazed over the busy market. To Lana, he appeared to be watching the masses of tourists with a mixture of awe and disdain. Water poured out of the rocks and into a large basin surrounding the mythical figures' feet. In the shallow pool, the water appeared to be more green than blue.

Buildings painted in soft yellows and oranges lined one side of the square, contrasting nicely with the Sant'Agnese in Agone, an ivory white church situated on the other. In front of that masterpiece of baroque architecture stood a Christmas tree at least five stories tall wrapped in lights and dusted in artificial snow. Based on the sunny blue skies and mild temperatures, Lana doubted they ever got much of the real thing in this part of Italy.

"Do you see any nativity scenes that are about three feet wide?" Dotty pushed, bringing her attention back to the task at hand. "That would block out the base of my tree."

"No, I don't see anything bigger than a foot," Lana replied. "Besides, how would we get something that big back to Seattle without it breaking?"

"You do have a point," Dotty said, her tone divulging her disappointment.

Lana scanned the cramped stall again until her eyes rested on a manger scene big enough to please her boss, yet compact enough to fit into a suitcase.

"What about this one?" She aimed her phone's camera towards the intricate scene, took a photo, and sent it to her boss.

"It's perfect—I can see baby Jesus's face! Add it to the pile," Dotty squealed.

Lana turned to the shopkeeper, already busy packing up their other purchases, and pointed to the nativity scene. "We'll take that one, too."

The man's grin intensified as he carefully lifted the massive object from the shelf. When he rang it up at the register, Lana startled at the hefty price, glad that her boss had given her permission to charge it all to the company credit card.

Randy whispered in her ear. "If Dotty keeps this up, we'll need to take a taxi back to the hotel."

Lana eyed the Christmas decorations, figurines, and nativity scene they had chosen and nodded in agreement. There were at least twenty pieces on the counter that still had to be wrapped for transport.

"I heard that, Randy," Dotty called out. "Get yourself a taxi and I'll pack an extra suitcase so I can get it all back to Seattle in one piece. I do appreciate you doing this for me. Those Italian decorations are so unique, I know they will be the perfect gifts for my good friends and family. I should have planned more time in Rome so I could have shopped for them myself."

"They really do have a gorgeous selection of decorations here," Lana agreed. She had already purchased several hangers shaped like the Colosseum and Saint Peter's Basilica. However, her favorites were the ornaments featuring "La Befana," a big-nosed, broom-riding witch who brings presents to Italian children on January 6. Lana had gotten several for her own friends and family. Like Dotty, she was glad to be able to give them something unique on Christmas Day.

"It's not a problem, Dotty. We're just surprised by the quantity, that's all," Randy teased his boss. "How many friends do you have, anyway?"

"I know it's a lot, but I don't want anyone to feel left out. Which reminds me—could you pick up one more ornament? Something manly—maybe Randy can choose it for me," Dotty said.

"Sure," he said and began scanning the wares for another gift.

"What's going on? Do you have a new boyfriend?" Lana teased, expecting

3

her boss to laugh off her remark.

"Yes, well, I do have a new man in my life, and I want to get him something special."

Lana's mouth dropped open. "Oh, yeah—what's he like? How tall is he? Is he retired? Is he handsome?"

"Hush, child, you're making me blush. He is quite tall and a true gentleman. You'll meet him at Randy's wedding next week."

"It must be serious if he's flying over with you."

"We are getting pretty close, that's true," Dotty said, her tone noncommittal.

"That's great; I'm happy for you."

Her boss, six times a widower, had been single for the past two years and, as far as Lana knew, had not been on the lookout for a new partner. Lana couldn't blame her. Though all of Dotty's marriages had been happy ones, her husbands did have an unfortunate tendency to die soon after they tied the knot. Not that Dotty was a black widow. In fact, all of her husbands had been killed when she was nowhere near them. Lana wasn't certain how all six had passed, but knew that one had been trampled by elephants in India, another had been knocked off a sailboat during a Seattle storm, and a third had sustained shark bites while diving in Fiji. She hoped whoever Dotty had her sights set on next was luckier and less accident-prone than her other husbands.

Dotty whispered through the phone, "Hey, Lana—how is Randy holding up?"

Lana took the call off speaker and stepped away from her fellow guide. "Randy is a bundle of nerves. But who wouldn't be, a week before their wedding day?"

"I sure hope leading that tour through Naples didn't make things worse."

Lana looked to Randy and considered Dotty's question as she reviewed the ten-day tour in her mind. She and Randy had just completed a fascinating tour of Naples, including excursions to Vesuvius, Pompeii, and Herculaneum. After they'd gotten their guests to the airport this morning, they'd jumped on a train and headed north to Rome.

"He was a bit jittery the first night, but as soon as the tour started, he was in his element. He did a great job guiding, as usual, and was his normal jovial self almost all of the time. If anything, the guests' questions helped keep him distracted from the week ahead. Gloria did call quite a few times with questions about the wedding, some of which he couldn't answer. It is a good thing that he is able to go to her family's village a few days before it takes place. They have so much to get ready before their big day. And by working this tour, he's had time to adjust to the time zone so he won't have to deal with jet lag when meeting Gloria's extended family for the first time."

Randy had told Gloria, when she'd accepted his proposal, that he wanted to make her ideal wedding come true. He didn't realize at the time that her perfect day included getting married in a foreign country. Her dream of exchanging nuptials in the same village that her parents had was incredibly romantic, but did create a few extra hurdles they would not have had to deal with if they had married in Seattle.

"That's true. I'm glad to hear it. Why don't you—" Dotty's voice was momentarily drowned out by barking. Seconds later, she yelled out, "Chipper! Rodney! You leave Seymour alone."

"Dotty? Are you still there?"

"I'm sorry, Lana. My boys are having fun chasing your cat around. But I promise they haven't actually caught him. Seymour is one fast feline," Dotty said, admiration in her voice.

"Don't worry, I know they are just having fun." Lana knew from experience that Dotty's pug and Jack Russell terrier loved to chase after her cat, but that Seymour was always several steps ahead.

"Mary Sue is moving in tomorrow, so she can get used to the boys' routine before I leave."

"That's great. I'm so glad your new tenant is also able to look after our pets while we're in Italy. Is she nice?"

"She seems pleasant enough but doesn't have much spunk. I'll have to work on that. But don't worry, Lana, she could never replace you," Dotty rushed to add.

"You're sweet. I miss our chats, too."

"Hey, thanks a bunch for picking up all of those presents for me," Dotty said. "Treat yourself to a nice dinner tonight—on me."

"That's really generous of you," Lana said as she looked at her watch. "Gosh, we'd better pay for these and grab a cab. It's already three in the afternoon. No wonder my stomach is rumbling."

"You two take care. I'll see you next week," Dotty sang out before hanging up.

2

Enough Bad Luck For A Lifetime

December 18—Day One of the Wanderlust Tour in Rome, Italy

A loud knocking caused Lana's eyes to spring open.

"Lana, are you awake?" Randy shouted through her hotel room door. "My friends are here!"

"Yep, I'm up," she responded in an equally loud voice as she kicked her legs over the side of the bed. According to her world clock, it was seven in the morning. After ten days of rising early, Lana had been looking forward to sleeping in. Randy's friends' arrival had put the kibosh on that.

"We'll be downstairs in the breakfast room. Why don't you join us after you've freshened up?"

"Sounds great," Lana said and stretched her arms out over her head. "I'm going to jump in the shower and I'll be down in fifteen minutes."

"No rush. They just arrived."

"Thanks for letting me know, Randy. See you soon."

Lana rushed anyway, driven by a need for caffeine as well as a desire to see Randy's fiancée and friends again. She'd met all of them at different parties and hiking trips over the past year, and enjoyed their company.

Randy had invited several friends to attend his Christmas Eve wedding in Tuscany, though he had expected most to bow out because of the travel costs. To his delight, many had agreed to come. Unfortunately, a few of his best friends had also expressed an interest in seeing more of Italy before the wedding. Because of the international location, Randy really needed that time to help his fiancée put the finishing touches on their wedding. He'd felt as if he had to choose between getting ready for his big day or entertaining his friends.

Luckily their boss had stepped in and offered to set up a three-day budget tour of Rome for his pals, in order to free up Randy's time. Seeing as she was dating Randy's older brother, Alex, Lana had also planned to come to Rome for the wedding. And that was also why Dotty felt that she was the natural choice to lead Randy's laid-back friends around the city. Lana was thrilled at the chance to spend some time sightseeing in Rome, as well as get to know his friends even better. In comparison to the wealthier and somewhat demanding clients she usually accompanied on these trips, leading them around was going to be a cinch.

After showering, Lana pulled on slacks and a loose-fitting blouse, knowing she needn't worry about dressing to impress. To most of Randy's friends, wearing a clean T-shirt and long pants was formal enough. She did hesitate at her choice of a short-sleeved top, but one look outside confirmed her selection was appropriate. The sun was already out, and there wasn't a cloud in the sky. Lana could hardly believe it was the second week of December. A sunny, seventy-degree day felt downright balmy, especially compared to Seattle's cold and wet winters.

When she entered the breakfast room, Randy and his friends cheered. They were all seated around a long table, and most were wearing matching jackets made of a shiny black fabric. On the back was an outline of Mount Rainier with the Space Needle in front of it and "Straight Up Climbs" embroidered underneath.

"Great to see you," Gloria squealed and rose to squeeze her tight. She looked so pretty in her sky blue dress with her springing curls dancing around her shoulders; she was certainly going to be a beautiful bride.

"You, too. Alex sends his love. He really regrets not being here for the preparty."

"It's okay. We understand that he'd already committed to working this week. At least he'll be here for the wedding. How is it, living with Alex? He is quite a neat freak."

"Yes, well, I am, too, so it all works out." Lana blushed as she reviewed the past three glorious months in her mind. It was so easy living with Alex, she felt as if they had already been together for years. "It's wonderful. I'm glad we decided to go for it."

Gloria squeezed her shoulder. "You just wait, I wouldn't be surprised if Alex pops the question before you two leave Italy. We're going to be sisters-in-law before you know it!"

"Whoa—we only moved in together a few months ago. There's no need to rush things. Please don't give him any ideas."

Lana turned back to the rest, hoping Gloria would let this nonsense about getting engaged go. "Hey—nice jackets!" she exclaimed.

"We have one for you, too," Randy said as he presented her with a small bag. "Welcome to the Straight Up club."

Inside was the same coat. She pulled it on, reveling in the silky softness of the fabric against her skin. It wasn't warm but loose and roomy with a water-resistant coating. "Excellent, this is perfect for the weather here. My winter jacket is way too warm."

"That's great. And this way everybody will know we're a group," Heather laughed. The petite blonde was one of Randy's oldest friends and the definition of a bubbly personality. Lana knew they had known each other since childhood and also worked together at Straight Up, where Heather was responsible for the climbing equipment and supplies.

"Oh yeah, I should check mine," Gloria said, pulling on the same jacket, albeit one that was more worn than Lana's new one. "Phew—mine still fits! I wasn't certain it would, to be honest."

It took Lana a moment to process Gloria's comment. "That's right—I forgot you that you and Randy met when you both worked for Straight Up. Why did you leave the company?"

Randy's smile faltered, but Gloria's remained in place. "Shortly after I started working there, a girlfriend of mine made me an offer I couldn't refuse." She chuckled at her *Godfather* reference as Randy groaned.

"She started an all-woman guide team, and working with them is fabulous! If you ever want to base yourself out of Seattle, you should apply for a job there." Gloria turned to the partially bald man sitting next to Heather. "Hey, Craig, let's see how your jacket looks. I hope we picked the right size for you."

"Gosh, let me check." Craig stared at his for a moment before tentatively sticking one plump arm into a sleeve. He was the only one of Randy's friends not dressed in a T-shirt and jeans. Considering he was an architect, Lana figured he was more used to wearing the suit and tie that he had on than the casual clothes the rest were wearing. Lana had briefly chatted with him a few times before, but he was quite subdued and rather shy, meaning she hadn't gotten to know him as well as the others. When he did finally slide the jacket on, Lana noticed that it was a bit too big for him.

Randy pulled out a chair for Lana. "What can I get you to drink?"

"A latte would be heavenly right now."

"Coming up. Gloria, darling, would you mind assisting me for a moment? I want to get everyone another round."

"I'm happy to help, but I'm definitely not your assistant," she teased as she slapped Randy's backside and sauntered off to the coffee machine.

"I do love that woman—she's so feisty." Randy gazed adoringly at his wife-to-be before joining her.

Lana really liked Gloria, too. She was laid-back, yet not a pushover, and quite funny when she wasn't stressed out. She took her seat and turned to Katherine, an administrative assistant at Straight Up Climbs, and her boyfriend, Bruce.

"Hey, there! It's been a long time. I haven't seen you two since Randy's birthday back in May. How are you?"

"We're doing great," Katherine said softly, making sideways eye contact with Lana. As nice as she was, Katherine was one of the shyest and most withdrawn people Lana had ever met. Her boyfriend, on the other hand, was gregarious and always smiling. In their cases, opposites really did attract.

Bruce leaned forward to better make eye contact with Lana. "We bought a cabin on Bainbridge Island a few months ago. It's tiny, but the views of the

Seattle skyline are incredible at night. But we've been so busy fixing it up, we haven't had much time to party."

"That sounds wonderful. Bainbridge Island is one of my favorite places to paddle."

"You and Alex will have to bring your kayaks over and we'll all go out on the water together," Bruce said as he wrapped his arm around his girlfriend's shoulder and pulled her close. "What do you say, Kat?"

"That sounds great. I'll take any excuse to get out on the water. That's why we wanted to move over to the island," she said as she smiled up lovingly at her boyfriend.

"We aren't quite used to the ferry system yet, but luckily my boss has been pretty relaxed about my tardiness, so far," Bruce guffawed. "He's even letting me work from home twice a week, at least until we finish renovating the cabin."

"I'm jealous. Straight Up isn't as accommodating. But I haven't been late to work once," Katherine rushed to add as she made eye contact with Heather, who worked for the same company.

"That must be so wonderful to wake up to the sounds of waves and seagulls," Lana said dreamily.

"It is, though it took us a while to get used to the quietness at night," Bruce replied. "We lived on the Seattle waterfront for so long I actually miss hearing trolleys, cars, and buses driving by at all hours."

"I found a store that sells samples of traffic noise recorded in different cities. It's really helping us both with the transition," Katherine said, adding with a laugh, "We've found New York to be the best one so far."

Heather burst out laughing. "What do you mean, like taxis beeping and pedestrians cursing?"

"Exactly. It's pretty funny, actually," Bruce said, "and really effective. I'm glad Katherine found it." He squeezed his girlfriend's shoulder, getting another tender smile in return.

"Watch out—hot drinks coming through!" Gloria called out as she set the first of two teas down in front of Katherine.

Heather jutted her elbows up onto the table, jostling their drinks, before

11

resting her chin on her hands. "Gosh, I would love to visit New York one day. It's too bad I hate to travel. It took all of my nerve and lots of Dramamine to fly over here. But I couldn't miss my best friend's wedding. Gloria, you are one lucky girl."

Randy grabbed Gloria's hand as a grin split his face in two. "Yes, she is." Gloria swatted his hand away. "Ha! Randy is the lucky one."

"After all the trouble you had with Rachel last year, I'm glad you found a nice, stable woman to settle down with," Craig said.

Gloria paled at the remark as Randy glowered at his friend. "What's wrong with you? Why would you bring her up?"

Craig slapped his hand against his forehead. "What am I, a doofus? I'm sorry about mentioning your ex. Lucky for you, she's ancient history. Cheers to Gloria and Randy," he said and hefted his cup up in the air. "After everything horrible that happened last year, you two deserve happiness."

Lana raised her glass, too, wondering what ex-girlfriend Craig was referring to. Randy had never mentioned anyone named Rachel.

Before she could ask, Craig continued, "Speaking of ancient history, Randy, do you remember Tammy Swartz? I ran into her at the airport! I hardly recognized her, but she recognized me."

"Oh, yeah, Tammy from college, right? Gosh, I haven't heard that name in years," Randy said before taking a swig of coffee and looking away.

Lana had a strong feeling that Randy was attempting to end the conversation, but Gloria wasn't ready to let it go. "Who is she? Randy's not mentioned a Tammy before."

A wave of irritation passed over Randy's face.

"She was my high school sweetheart. We were still dating when we started college, at least until she met Randy. She dumped me to date him," Craig said brightly as he looked to his friend, then shrugged. "Tammy and I had been drifting apart, anyway."

Gloria glared at her fiancé. "Why did you steal his girlfriend?"

Randy glowered at Craig. "I didn't know the two of them were dating until Tammy and I had already gone out a few times. We'd just started college, and I didn't know Craig that well yet. I stopped seeing her as soon as I found

12

out."

"Yeah, but by then it was too late, wasn't it?" Craig snickered. "It doesn't matter. She's happily married with two kids and a dog. I guess neither of us was the right one for her. Luckily, you've found your soul mate."

Yikes, Craig is in a nasty mood, Lana thought. Was he jet-lagged or perhaps a little jealous of Randy's luck with love? Fortunately, no one else seemed to notice.

"Say, Gloria, what can you tell us about this wedding?" Heather piped up. "From what Randy's said, it's costing him a fortune."

Gloria glared at Heather as Randy turned redder than a fire hydrant. Lana cringed at the young woman's callousness. *Heather is definitely not afraid to speak her mind*, she thought.

When Gloria opened her mouth to respond, Randy laid a hand on her arm. "It's okay. Heather must have misunderstood me. The wedding you want is the one that will make me happy, too—end of story," Randy soothed his fiancée before turning to the others.

"It is going to be a big wedding, but I'm not paying for all of it—Gloria's family and friends have done most of the work. They're making all of the decorations, food, and even the wine. All that's left for me to do is some grunt work—putting together the party tents and hanging up the lights, that kind of thing—and we'll be ready to go."

"That's incredibly kind of them! What can you tell us about it?" Lana asked.

Gloria's focus remained on Heather, but she answered Lana nonetheless. "Where to begin? My sister-in-law is making flower wreathes for the maids of honor. My aunts and grandmother have sewn their dresses, as well. Dad already bottled a Chianti Classico years ago that was meant to be served on my wedding day. I laughed at him at the time, but it's ripened quite nicely since then," Gloria chortled. "I only hope there is enough for all the guests."

"How many people did you invite?" Craig asked.

Gloria and Randy looked to each other and grinned. "Between our families and friends, we're expecting about two hundred people to attend," she said.

When Randy's friends' jaws dropped, he quickly added, "Gloria's granddad is active in his village and invited almost everyone who lives there. And both of our parents have several siblings with children, all of which are flying over. Luckily, Gloria's grandparents own a vineyard and are letting us transform their garden into an outdoor hall. It's a massive space, so we will have plenty of room to set up the tables and tents."

"Wow, I didn't realize you had invited so many people," Heather exclaimed, showing no signs of shame at her previous remarks. "It sounds like it's going to be a fun party."

"It should be, once we get everyone out to the vineyard. That will take a lot of taxi and bus rides, I bet." Randy winked at his fiancée.

"What is the name of this mystery village, anyway? I assume it's somewhere in Tuscany if we're getting out at Florence," Craig asked.

Randy stiffened, and his tone became guarded. "Why does it matter? You know we're keeping it a surprise until the big day."

When Craig threw his hands up, Randy's expression softened. "I have you all booked into a local hotel close to the vineyard. It looks really quaint; I think you'll like it. I just hope they have enough room for all of our out-of-town guests."

Gloria laughed. "They don't. Grandpa already talked several of his friends into taking the bigger families into their homes for the week. It seems like everyone on my side of the family has at least five kids."

"Watch out, Randy. Before you know it, you'll be stuck in Seattle changing diapers instead of traveling the world," Heather joked, or so Lana thought. Yet, the younger woman's tone and expression were quite serious.

"How are you two going to earn a living if you have kids, anyway? You're both guides working irregular hours. And Randy, you are abroad more than you're home these days," Heather pondered aloud. The rest stared at her with their mouths agape.

Heather threw a hand over hers when she noticed the rest staring at her. "Did I say that aloud? I'm sorry—my mouth sometimes runs when it should not. I'm going to go to the ladies' room." She jumped up and scampered away before anyone could respond.

"Great friend," Gloria growled at Heather's retreating figure. "Why did you invite her if she hates the fact that you're getting married?"

"I don't know what's gotten into her. She's never made any offensive remarks about you before. She means well, though she often forgets to filter what comes out of her mouth. The jet lag probably isn't helping."

"No wonder she's still single," Gloria huffed.

"Why don't you two give Heather a break? She just needs a little more time to get used to the idea of you two getting married, that's all," Craig said.

Randy stared at him. "What are you talking about?"

"Come on, Randy, she's been in love with you for years. Have you seriously never noticed?" Craig asked.

"What? No, she's like the little sister I never had. We've always had each other's backs, but there's never been any romantic tension between us."

"Are you sure? Maybe it's one sided," Gloria said.

"Do you really think that she is? Why haven't you said anything before?" Randy asked.

"What was I supposed to say? I had asked if you two had ever been in a relationship, and your emphatic no convinced me that you had not. But I never found the right moment to ask Heather if she was interested in you. And she does call you pretty much every day."

"Yeah, to check in and see how I'm doing. We haven't been meeting up as much as we used to, but then again, we don't work together anymore." Randy blew out his cheeks and shook his head. "I can't believe this. What am I supposed to do—go and comfort her? Or will that give her the wrong signal? I don't want to lose her friendship, but I don't want to give her false hope that we'll ever be together, either."

Though Randy was looking to Gloria for the answer, Craig responded instead. "Give her a few minutes alone. Lana or Gloria can always fetch her if she's not back by the time we want to leave."

"Craig's right. Just let her be for now," Gloria added.

"I agree with the others that you should give her some space. But I don't think she's in love with you," Katherine said in her quiet voice.

Lana was momentarily puzzled by Katherine's assertion, until she recalled that the three of them had worked together at Straight Up Climbs for several years. She would have had more chances to observe their relationship than

Craig.

"Before you met Gloria, you and Heather used to go biking and hiking most weekends," Katherine explained. "But since you two have started dating, I haven't heard Heather mention you two taking any trips together. And now that you're getting married, you'll probably have even less time for her. I bet Heather just needs some time to get used to how you're not available to hang out as much. You two have known each other forever."

Randy nodded slowly. "Sorry, Craig, but I think Katherine's pegged this one. Heather does like to keep in touch, but she's never made a move on me. And she's had plenty of chances to try over the years." He stood up, as if making clear that this topic was closed for discussion. "Does anyone want anything else to eat before we go?"

"I don't need any more food, but I do have a pressing question for the bride-to-be before we leave." Lana leaned in towards Gloria. "Randy said your grandmother is making your dress. I'm dying to know what it looks like."

Gloria pulled out her phone, Heather already forgotten. "Here's a photo of me in it during our last fitting."

It was an off-the-shoulder gown with a full skirt and long trail of embroidered silk running down the back. Lana could imagine her grandmother had spent weeks sewing the details into the waist and neckline.

"Wow, that is amazing! You look like an angel. Your grandmother is quite the accomplished seamstress," Lana exclaimed.

When Randy leaned over to take a look, Gloria quickly turned the phone away. "Hey! You're not supposed to see me in my wedding dress before the big day. It brings bad luck."

Randy paled. "Does it? I'm sorry, honey. We sure don't need any more of that, do we? Not after all we've gone through this past year. Look, the dress isn't finished yet, so I bet me seeing you in it doesn't count. Right?"

Gloria glared at her fiancé for a moment, and then her expression softened. "Let's hope so. We've already dealt with enough bad luck for a lifetime."

3

Iconic Monuments

"So what's on the itinerary today?" Craig asked Randy after Heather returned from the ladies' room.

"I figure we should start with the most iconic monument in the city."

"Do you mean the Vatican?" Heather responded.

Randy frowned. "No, I meant the Colosseum, but you make a great point. Lana will take you to the Vatican Museums and Saint Peter's Basilica later this week. Because Gloria's parents are arriving in a few hours, I thought it would be better to see some of the archeological ruins instead. You're going to need the whole day to see the Vatican."

"Ooh, I can't wait to see the Colosseum. I've always wanted to get a picture taken with one of those gladiators you see hanging around the entrance," Katherine said shyly.

"I'm sorry to have to tell you this, but the gladiators aren't allowed to pose for pictures in front of the Colosseum anymore," Lana explained as gently as she could. Katherine was one of those people who seemed almost afraid to speak her mind, and Lana felt bad that when she finally did, she had to disappoint her.

"Oh," Katherine replied and bit her lip.

"Why not?" Bruce asked as he wrapped an arm around his girlfriend. He was extremely protective of her, Lana noted, which was probably for the best. She needed a little extra protecting.

"Apparently many of them were charging exorbitant amounts for a single photo and then intimidating and threatening tourists when they refused to pay. Some were even caught picking their clients' pockets!"

"That's really too bad," Heather said. "I was looking forward to seeing them, too."

"You can always take a picture with one of us boys at the gladiator school tonight," Bruce said exuberantly while flexing his muscles.

Craig glared at Bruce while nodding towards Randy. "Hey, I thought that was supposed to be a surprise."

"I know the groom isn't supposed to know what he's doing for his bachelor party, but I had to make sure he was still going to be in Rome before I booked it. They don't offer refunds and it's pretty pricey," Bruce explained before quickly adding, "But you're worth it, Randy. It's going to be great!"

"It's a good thing you did ask him before we booked our train tickets," Gloria said. "Randy was going to travel with my parents and me to our family's vineyard this afternoon."

"But a stag party is worth sticking around for," Randy added. "I mean, how many times does a man get married?"

"Statistically speaking, two and a half. Fifty-four percent of first marriages end in divorce—that's more than half. The chances of success decline significantly for the second and third marriages," Heather said in an emotionless voice.

Lana puffed out her cheeks as she stared at the young woman. *What is wrong with Heather?* She'd always been so bubbly and outgoing at Randy's parties. But this Heather seemed bitter and angry. Was she in love with Randy, or did she just need a chance to adjust to this new dynamic? Whatever her reasoning, Lana hoped Heather would call a truce with Gloria. If she didn't, Lana doubted Randy would want to keep in touch after he got married.

"Besides," Randy continued, ignoring Heather, "Jake isn't arriving until tonight. This way, I can spend time with him, too, before the wedding frenzy kicks in."

"Hey." Gloria poked an elbow into her fiancé's ribs.

Randy laughed and kissed her forehead. "You know I'm only teasing. I can't wait to get married to you." He pulled her in for a passionate kiss—one that made the rest of the table blush simultaneously and avert their gazes.

Lana racked her brain, trying to recall Jake's face. He was one of Randy's newer friends, a young man he'd recently met through mutual acquaintances. All Lana could recall was that Jake was as passionate about rock climbing as Randy was. And thanks to Randy's recommendation, Jake had recently gotten a job as a guide for Straight Up Climbs.

"It's too bad Alex couldn't make it in time for the bachelor party," Craig said.

"I know that he is sorry, too," Lana answered. "He was looking forward to getting silly with you all."

Randy brushed it off. "Alex had committed to working at that conference before Gloria and I decided to tie the knot on Christmas Eve. I understand completely. I'm just glad he can make it to the wedding. I wouldn't want to get married without him being there to witness it. Besides, he is my best man."

"Trust me, the feeling is mutual. He will be there." Lana knew that the Wright brothers were extremely close and that Alex wouldn't be able to live with himself if he somehow missed Randy's wedding. He was already mad enough that his boss wouldn't let him take the week off, but the team was shorthanded at the moment. Alex had little choice but to stay if he wanted to remain employed.

"Alex should be arriving a few hours before Dotty flies over from Seattle, which means we can all ride the train to Florence together."

One of the hotel's receptionists burst into the breakfast hall and scanned the room. When she spotted Randy, she strode over to him. "Excuse me, sir, but your taxi is here."

"Oh! Gosh, is it ten o'clock already? Hey gang, it's time to start our day. Is everyone ready?"

He looked to his friends and got a round of nods in response.

"Watch out, Rome, here we come!"

19

4

World At Your Fingertips

Standing atop the upper levels of the ancient Colosseum, Lana felt as if she'd been transported back to Roman times. *These would have been the cheap seats,* she realized as she stared down the three levels of seating towards the oval-shaped podium below. The gladiators must have seemed tiny from up here, she reckoned.

This stone amphitheater, built around 70 AD by emperors of the Flavian dynasty, was the largest in the Roman world. Here gladiators had once been forced to fight; wild animals, pitted against each other; and naval battles, reenacted. When it was first built, there was room for fifty thousand spectators. Time and robbers had worn it down, but the structure was still incredibly impressive and quite large.

From her lofty position, she could see the top of the Arch of Constantine and many stone pines, the tall umbrella-like trees Rome was famous for. She looked through the iconic curved windows at the puffy white clouds racing overhead, the window framing the scene perfectly. It was truly magical simply standing here, high up on this ancient structure.

They had begun their day in the Roman Forum—the remnants of an ancient neighborhood built several feet under Rome's current street level. Lana couldn't keep her eyes off of the stoic columns that once graced the Temple of Saturn, now standing forlorn as the building behind it no longer existed. It was not always easy to visualize all of the important government buildings that once filled the massive space, but their guide did her best to describe the streets' layout and explain the purpose of each structure.

Their strolling pace was great for soaking up the sun as well as watching Randy's friends interact. Lana had only talked to them at parties or on hikes; she hadn't socialized with them otherwise.

Luckily, once they'd left the hotel, their petty squabbles had been forgotten, and the group of friends was clearly enjoying seeing the sights together. She was glad the normal tensions and irritations that she usually had to deal with during a tour weren't going to be an issue this week.

There were, however, far more displays of affection than she was used to. Randy and Gloria took every opportunity to sneak kisses, which Lana expected from a couple about to be married. However, Bruce and Katherine's cuddling and smooching did surprise her, seeing as how reserved Katherine was. Both pairs were so cute together and obviously enjoying being in this romantic city that it didn't bother her, but it did make her miss Alex even more. She was so glad he would be flying into Rome in time to travel to Tuscany with the rest. *If only he'd been able to find a colleague to switch with him so he could have been here for the entire trip,* Lana mused, although she recognized that it was neither of the Wright brothers' fault that the timing ended up as it did.

After they exited the Colosseum and were trying to get their bearings, a young mother pushing two screaming babies passed close by their group. The young woman was chattering to her children in Italian, her high-pitched voice increasing in volume as she walked, yet nothing seemed to calm the babies down. Gloria went over to the harried mother, cooing at the infants until they stopped crying. As the two women talked, the mother obviously grateful to Gloria for her help, Lana noticed how pale Randy had become.

She caught his eye and moved in closer. "Everything okay?"

"Yeah, I guess." He gulped as he watched his fiancée warily. "What if Heather is right? Gloria and I have talked about wanting to have kids someday, but not about when or how we would manage it with the jobs we have. What if she wants to start a family right away? How would we survive financially? I haven't worked as anything but a guide since I graduated from college. If we have children, I don't want to be on the road more than I am at home. But how are we going to pay the rent otherwise?"

Lana smiled gently at her friend, wishing she knew how to calm him down. She was ten years older than Randy, yet had never had the opportunity to have children. Her ex-husband was against it, and she and Alex had never talked about having them.

"Oh, Randy. You're only twenty-eight years old! You have the world at your fingertips. Besides, it's normal to get cold feet right before your wedding day. I understand you're feeling uncertain, but I would wait to talk to Gloria about kids until after you're married. Doing so now would just stress you both out."

Randy nodded glumly.

"Hey, it's all going to work out. The most important thing is you know you want to be with Gloria. That's all that matters right now. You'll have plenty of chances to talk about the rest later, preferably after your honeymoon."

Randy squeezed her shoulder. "Thanks, Lana. You are a true friend."

5

Meet the Parents

"Before we head back to the hotel, there's one place I always visit when I'm in Rome," Gloria said. "It's become a tradition, I guess. It's close by; follow me."

She led them towards the back of the Colosseum where a steep set of stairs took them up to the busy street circling the ancient amphitheater. Gloria navigated their way across the chaotic traffic and further into the adjoining neighborhood. Soon they were standing in front of a simple structure made of red-brown bricks with a curious bell tower rising high above it. Lana hadn't quite seen anything like it before. Built into the skinny tower were six openings, seemingly held up by white columns. Lana could imagine the views were incredible.

"Santa Maria in Cosmedin is a Byzantine church built in the eighth century," Gloria explained as she led them through the entrance and around to the back of the structure. "It's interesting, but the church itself is not why I wanted to come here. It's because of this."

She pointed towards a large disc mounted under a portico on the outside wall of the church. As they walked closer, the vague outline of an old, wizened man with long hair and a beard seemed to appear on its surface. The man's mouth was open wide, as if he was captured midyawn. A short line of tourists were waiting to get close to the figure, which was cordoned off by a velvet rope. Lana startled when she realized those at the head of the line were daring each other to place their hands inside of the figure's mouth.

"What are those people doing? Should we call security?" Lana asked. After visiting so many gorgeous sites around Europe, she'd become quite short-tempered with those callous enough to use ancient relics as their background for selfies. Those kinds of visitors were usually so concerned with the framing of their shots, they damaged priceless objects through their carelessness.

Gloria laughed as she ushered them towards the back of the line. "No, we don't need to call anyone. This is the Bocca della Verità, the Mouth of Truth. You're supposed to put your hand into its mouth—if you dare!"

When she began cackling, the rest looked at her as if she was crazy. Gloria gestured towards the massive disc. "Scholars think that it is an ancient lie detector. When my dad brought me here for the first time, he pinched my leg when I put my hand in that thing's mouth and scared me so badly that I peed my pants!"

Randy laughed along, but the others stared at her blankly.

"Why were you afraid to put your hand in its mouth?" Lana asked.

"Legend has it that it bites the hands off of liars," Randy explained.

Heather sprung out of line. "Count me out. I'm too superstitious to go anywhere near that thing."

"What's wrong? Are you really afraid it's going to bite your hand off? What have you been lying about, anyway?" Randy teased.

Heather looked towards the ground as her face flushed red.

"There's no proof it really does close, right?'" Lana reasoned.

"I don't care. I'm not taking any chances," Heather said before leaving them and entering the church.

Gloria raised an eyebrow at Randy, who shrugged in return. "I have no idea what is going on with her. Heather just isn't herself this week."

After the rest had taken turns testing their mettle, Randy checked his watch. "Sorry, folks, but it's time to get a taxi back to the hotel. Gloria's parents should be arriving any minute, and I don't want to upset them—especially a few days before I marry their daughter."

Gloria laughed. "No, you definitely don't want to make them wait for you. It drives my dad crazy."

Their taxi driver raced them back to the hotel, honking and shouting at any scooters or passersby who dared block his path. Yet as soon as they walked into the hotel, Gloria's parents rushed over to them.

"There you are!" Gloria's mother said as she wrapped her daughter up in a bear hug.

"Oh, no. I'm so sorry we're late, Mom," Gloria cried.

"Don't sweat it, pumpkin. Our plane was on time and by some miracle your dad's bags didn't get lost, so we are early for a change."

Lana loved listening to Gloria's parents speak. They had grown up in the village Gloria and Randy were to marry in, and emigrated to Seattle thirty years ago. Although they both spoke perfect English, there were glorious hints of their melodious accent still present in their speech.

"Great to see you, Randy." Her father held out a hand.

"Yes, sir. You, too. I hope you had a good flight."

Lana hid a smile behind her hand as Randy straightened up and his tone became more formal.

"It was, but stop with the sir, okay? Call me Dad. We're practically family—or will be in a few days' time," Gloria's father admonished.

"Okay, Dad. Do you want to eat something before we head over to the train station? Or would you prefer to walk around and see the sights?" Randy reddened as he stumbled over his words.

The older man looked at his watch. "I think it's best if we left for the station now. We can eat lunch on the train. Are you all packed up, Gloria?"

She rolled her eyes. "The train doesn't leave for two hours!"

"But our taxi might get a flat tire," her dad reasoned. "Besides, you can never be too early. Isn't that right, Randy?"

"Yes, sir," he responded, correcting himself when the older man looked at him sternly. "I mean, Dad. You're right. Gloria is all packed. We can leave whenever you want."

"He's a keeper," Gloria's mother whispered to her daughter, loudly enough for all to hear.

"Gloria, why don't you get your bag and we'll head out," her father said.

Lana couldn't believe that they hadn't even acknowledged her or the

25

rest. Considering how friendly they usually were, Lana figured they were incredibly nervous about their daughter's upcoming nuptials.

"Hey, before you go—congratulations!"

Lana squeezed in between the family to hug Gloria's mother. They'd only met a few times, but she was always kind to Lana.

"Oh, Lana honey, you're such a sweetie. How rude of me not to say hello. It's great to see you, too. We're a little stressed out right now, but I'm glad we'll have time to catch up during our stay in Tuscany. Thanks for taking care of Randy's friends for a few days."

The older woman turned to the rest, a sheepish expression on her face. "It is good to see all of you. Thanks for letting us steal Randy away. We sure can use his help getting Gloria's dream wedding set up. Did Gloria tell you that the whole village chipped in to help make the food and decorations? Isn't that sweet?"

"She did mention that," Katherine said. "It's really nice of everyone to help make Randy and Gloria's wedding day even more special."

"It does take a lot of pressure off of Randy and me," Gloria added. "I didn't realize how much work it was going to be getting everything ready! I do wish I could stay and hang out with you guys, but I am looking forward to seeing all of my cousins and aunts again. Since we're leaving for our honeymoon the day after the wedding, I won't have much time to catch up with them before we fly to Egypt."

"Phew, I'm glad you're not bailing on us today," Gloria's mom said. "Your grandmother would murder me if you don't come up with us. She's worried she might have made the bodice too tight and needs you to try your dress on again so she has time to adjust it before the wedding."

Gloria grimaced. "I hope not. I'm going to need to breathe normally that day, otherwise I might faint. Lord knows I'll be nervous enough! Let me go get my bag and then we'll head out."

A few minutes later, Gloria reappeared with her luggage, and she, her parents, and Randy headed out to catch a cab. Randy turned to his friends as he reached the door. "Well, folks, I'll see you in a few hours. For now, I'm leaving you in Lana's capable hands."

6

Who is Rachel?

After the taxi drove off, Lana turned to Randy's friends. "You have got my curiosity piqued. Before Randy gets back, who is Rachel?"

Everyone fell silent and averted their gaze, discomfort etched across their faces. All except Heather, who let out a snort before responding. "I'm not surprised Randy didn't mention her—she destroyed his life."

Lana's brows crinkled in confusion.

"That's a great question for Kat," Bruce finally said, nodding to his girlfriend, who was standing stock still.

Moments later, Katherine let out a sigh, then locked eyes with Lana for the first time since they had arrived in Rome. The expression on her face was a mix of defiance and irritation. "Rachel is my older sister, for starters. She and Randy dated for three months, and according to Rachel, they are soul mates. Unfortunately for her, Randy didn't agree and dumped her because she was too needy."

When Katherine paused and looked away, Lana swore she saw a small smile forming on the woman's lips.

Lana's eyes widened as she tried to control her emotions, surprised that Randy was still good friends with the younger sister of a woman who had caused him so much pain.

"Rachel got a bit too obsessed with Randy, that's all," Craig offered in Rachel's defense. "She never meant to scare him. She's a good person, deep down, and she can be the nicest person you've ever met—"

"When it suits her needs," Katherine added.

"Randy thinks Rachel caused his fall into that crevasse," Heather piped up.

"You mean the one that shattered his leg?" Lana asked. "He'd always said it was an accident, so I thought he meant there was no one to blame."

"No one could prove she'd done it, but Rachel should have been on the ladder when it collapsed—not Randy," Heather said. "Sorry, Katherine, I know she's your sister. But she got away with attempted murder."

"It's okay. We aren't close. Although I still don't think she was involved."

"Randy was on too many painkillers when he made those accusations," Craig cut in. "Why would Rachel tamper with her own ladder?"

"Because she was already planning on faking her illness so that Randy would have to take her place," Heather insisted. "She must have bent that ladder's latch before she left. It was sabotage, Craig—no question about it."

"I don't know," he replied. "Rachel trying to harm him physically makes no sense. She wanted to date him again, not put him in the hospital. I think Randy was angry and looking for someone to blame. He'd just lost his livelihood and was really hurting inside."

"How can you say that?" Heather cried. "Especially considering all she did to make Randy's life a nightmare. They'd just had a big fight, and Randy threatened to go to the police if she didn't leave him be. She must have seen her chance to get back at him and took it. Rachel is so twisted; she probably wanted him to be hospitalized so that she could play nurse. The hospital's security did have to remove her from his room several times."

Craig sighed heavily and started to retort when Katherine held up her hand, effectively halting the discussion.

"It doesn't matter what any of us think—no one could prove that the ladder had been tampered with, and the rest of Rachel's gear was in tip-top shape. The authorities did have questions about the way Heather cleaned some of the equipment, but the insurance company proved that her work was perfect," Katherine said, eyeing her coworker through slitted lids.

"You better believe it was all in perfect working order. I know a faulty piece of equipment could cost a guide or client their life," Heather said. "I always give the gear a thorough cleaning after a guide brings it back to the shed. If I had seen that the latch was loose or damaged, I would have replaced it. That ladder was safe to use when Rachel took it out—I'd stake my life on it."

"Shed?" Lana asked.

"We used to keep the gear in a spare room in the main office building, but we've grown so much that I needed more space to store and clean it all. So we built a separate building next to the main office that we jokingly call the shed. It's not that big, but is large enough for my purposes."

Lana nodded in understanding. "So it wasn't Rachel's personal gear, but a piece of equipment anyone in the company could have used. I can understand why the insurance company didn't hold her accountable. But why did Randy take her place at the last minute?"

"She'd drawn the short straw and had to lug a ladder up to Disappointment Cleaver. Our guides usually place them over the larger crevasses as a convenience to other mountaineers, and to make sure the routes don't get backed up with traffic," Heather explained. "It's a tough climb and was Rachel's least favorite."

"How do you know that?" Craig challenged.

"Because she complained about it whenever she had to lead a group up that route," Heather snapped back.

"She and a new guide had just set off with the ladder when she suddenly raced back to the office and started throwing up," Katherine added. "I heard her tell our boss that she'd eaten something the night before that didn't agree with her and she wanted to go home to rest. I bet she didn't want to do the work and lied to get out of it."

Heather rolled her eyes. "She lied about being sick, alright. But because she knew that Randy would have to take her place. That's why she sabotaged the ladder, so that it would break when he was on it."

"Is it even possible to cause a ladder to fail like that one did?" Lana asked both women.

Heather shrugged. "It's easy enough to do. You would only have to bend the latch enough so that it would catch if no one was on it, but wouldn't hold once someone put their entire weight on it. It would be almost impossible to detect after it failed, especially in Randy's case. The ladder got crushed, along with his leg, during the fall."

Katherine clicked her tongue in irritation. "Yeah, well, conspiracy theories aside, when Rachel returned to the office, Randy had just shown up for work and did end up taking her place. Unfortunately, the ladder's clasp was faulty, and Randy ended up getting hurt. I still don't think my sister sabotaged anything—it was simply bad luck."

"It should have been Rachel on that ladder," Heather mumbled.

"Anyway, now you know who Rachel is," Bruce said, laughing nervously as he glanced at Heather and Katherine, still locked in a staring contest.

"Okay, so after Randy broke up with her, Rachel had trouble accepting that it was over," Lana said, trying to make certain she understood the situation.

"Ha! That's putting it mildly," Heather exclaimed. "She stalked him for months. Randy had to get a restraining order to keep her away from him."

Lana's eyes grew wide. "Are you kidding me?" Randy was always so positive and upbeat—she'd had no idea of the torture he'd endured.

"Meeting Gloria is the best thing that's ever happened to him," Bruce said. "Which is why Randy is being so secretive about their wedding's location. They are doing everything they can to make certain she can't find out where it's going to be held. Did you guys know that Rachel started showing up in front of his house a few weeks before he left for Naples? She didn't get out of the car, but would beep and wave at him as she drove by."

Randy's friends shook their heads.

"That is creepy," Lana said. "Now I really understand why he didn't want her to know where the wedding is taking place."

"Exactly. I'm his oldest friend, and I don't even know," Craig said.

Heather punched his shoulder. "Hey, that honor is mine. I've known Randy since first grade."

Craig held up his hands in mock defense. "That's right. Sorry, I've only known him since freshman year of college."

"See—I've known him way longer," Heather gloated.

Lana wanted to laugh except for the seriousness on Heather's face. *What does it matter who knew Randy the longest?* she wondered.

Katherine leaned over towards Craig and Heather, a twinkle in her eye. "Okay, since you two have known Randy so long, tell us something about him that none of us know."

Heather opened her mouth to respond, but Craig beat her to it. "I've got a good one to share. During our sophomore year, we were walking back to our dorm after a party, and Randy decided to climb up onto the roof of the president's house! He made it up, but campus security arrived before he could get back down."

"What! Randy never told me about that," Heather said, slightly put out, while the rest laughed.

"Poor Randy, I can still see him hanging off that balcony with the security down below telling him to freeze," Craig chuckled along with the rest. "He spent a few hours in their custody, until the guards roused his parents out of their slumber and informed them of their son's youthful transgressions."

"Dad never did let me forget that," Randy piped up from behind them.

Heather jumped up and hugged him. "Hey, welcome back. That was fast."

Randy stepped out of her embrace. "Gloria insisted I get back to you all so we can see more of Rome together before Jake arrives and we mortal men become gladiators."

Randy stood wide and pounded on his chest, prompting Craig and Bruce to do the same.

Katherine shook her head. "I'm glad Gloria's not here to witness this manly display."

"Trust me, she would find it irresistible. What are you ladies going to do tonight?" Randy asked.

Lana looked to the other two women. "I took the liberty of booking us into a spa that's located in an ancient Roman bathhouse. I hope that's okay."

"Are you kidding me—that sounds wonderful!" Heather squealed.

Even Katherine grinned. "Great idea. Thanks, Lana."

7

The Spanish Steps

Lana marveled at the sight before her. From her position at the top of the Spanish Steps, it seemed as if all of Rome was spread out before her. Church domes sparkled in the morning light as the sun's rays cast the rest of the city in soft shades of salmon, peach, and tangerine.

When Randy led them down the first set of stairs to a small open terrace, Lana was taken aback by the massive nativity scene filling the space. They had seen many of these wonderfully detailed decorations during their walks around the city center, which helped remind her that it was Christmas, despite it being sunny and warm.

This one featured a street scene in what Lana assumed was Bethlehem, including carefully crafted replicas of buildings, market stalls, street vendors, palm trees, and a straw-filled shed topped by a golden comet. Inside, baby Jesus slept soundly in his manger while his parents and the three wise men looked on in adoration.

After they'd taken several photos of the extensive displays, Randy led them down to a half-sunken boat positioned at the bottom of the staircase and in the center of the Piazza di Spagna. Water poured out of both ends and flowed into a small basin.

"This is the Fontana della Barcaccia. Believe it or not, this fountain was Bernini's first assignment. He carved it with his dad, also a sculptor," Randy said.

Katherine frowned at the tiny boat. "Do you mean the famous sculptor Gian Lorenzo Bernini? The one who made so many of the baroque churches, palaces, and fountains we keep coming across on our walks?"

"Yep, one and the same."

Katherine eyed the leaking boat critically. "I guess we all have to start somewhere."

"That's true." Randy laughed.

"I like it," Heather said. "It's small yet charming."

"Indeed," Randy said, then gestured at a cream-colored building behind them. "And for you literary buffs, that is the Keats-Shelley Memorial House. The English poet John Keats died there."

"Ooh, I didn't know Babington's Tea Room was here," Craig said as he pointed to a small shop opposite the museum. "I promised my mom I would bring her back a bag of their tea. Does anyone else want to pick up something to take home?" he asked, then walked inside without waiting for an answer.

Heather and Bruce ambled over to the menu placed next to the door and scanned it. "Ouch, it's all too rich for my blood," Heather said.

Bruce nodded. "I'm with you, but it does look delicious."

Craig soon returned with two bags and a cookie in his mouth.

"These shortbread cookies are delicious. Any takers?"

"Yes, please," Katherine said.

Craig doled one out to all of his friends, then turned to Randy. "Where to next?"

"Our next stop is another fountain by Bernini and a chapel made of human bones."

"That sounds fantastic! Lead the way," Heather said as she locked arms with Randy. He smiled warmly down at his friend yet unwrapped his arm from her grip. Since Gloria had left for the train station, Heather had been clinging to Randy, and her extra attention was clearly making him uncomfortable. Maybe it was Craig and Gloria's remarks that made him question Heather's need for closeness. Or perhaps his impending nuptials were causing him to reevaluate his relationship with his female friends. Either way, Lana noted a distance that hadn't been there a few hours ago.

Randy led them a few blocks further to a busy intersection where a massive figure made of marble stood watch. The god Triton sat on a scallop shell resting on four dolphins' tails. He was holding a conch shell up to his mouth, from which a spurt of water shot up into the air. Rising behind it was the Hotel Bernini, presumably named in honor of the fountain's creator.

They crossed over the insanely busy intersection to reach the triangle-shaped space the intricately carved fountain was built on. When they approached the basin, Heather began to move towards Randy, but Lana got there first.

"I can't believe you're getting married! Thanks for letting me be Alex's plus one."

Randy turned to Lana, his tone sincere. "I wouldn't have wanted to get married without you being present."

"That's sweet," Lana said and blushed.

"I mean it—I owe you big time. When I started this job, I was so unsure about myself and what I was doing. You made me feel like I was good at being a city guide, which really boosted my confidence. I'm quite grateful, Lana."

"Oh, Randy. You're a natural; I didn't have to teach you anything."

"Still, I want you to know that you're not only a coworker or Alex's girlfriend; I also consider you a friend."

Honored and touched by his words, Lana wrapped him up in a hug.

"And if my brother gets his way, we'll officially be family before you know it."

"Hey!" Lana swatted his chest as she pulled away. "I don't need you pressuring me, as well."

Randy held up his hands. "Okay, but we both know that you're perfect for each other." He grinned wickedly, then called out, "Hey everybody, are you ready to see the bone chapel?"

8

Trevi Fountain

After a creepy yet fascinating visit to the Capuchin Crypt under the Santa Maria della Concezione dei Cappuccini church, a narrow space decorated with the bones of Capuchin friars, the group made their way further into the city center and towards the Trevi Fountain. Randy and Lana soon gave up trying to navigate the maze of streets via map and instead followed the large signs pointing to the city's most famous icons.

In many ways, the city center reminded Lana of most European cities, with a few major exceptions. She marveled at the open pits far below street level, in which the ruins of this ancient city were visible. Everywhere they walked, they passed marble statues and intricately carved mosaics that, in any other country, would be shut away in a museum and displayed behind glass. The chances of them being covered in graffiti, damaged, or stolen was too great.

Yet here, the locals used them as drying racks for their laundry, chairs for chatting with neighbors, and as a way to display their market goods. It was incredibly refreshing to see these beautiful designs and objects still so integrated into daily life.

What also astonished Lana was the number of fountains. You couldn't walk a block without encountering one—from a simple spout built into a wall, to an ornate, water-filled basin containing sculptures created by world-famous artists.

As they followed the signs for the Trevi, the sound of running water grew steadily louder, until they turned a tight corner and were suddenly confronted by a massive fountain built into the side of a block-long building. Water gushed out of multiple pipes into a basin the size of a small swimming pool. Lana took in the sculptures of gods and horses galloping over a rocky outcrop from which water flowed. It was phenomenal.

Randy stopped to admire the sight before them, a wide grin on his face. "This is Trevi Fountain, one of my favorite sights in the city." He had to raise his voice to be heard over the gushing water.

The narrow square in which they were standing was jam-packed with tourists jostling for the best positions to photograph this remarkable structure. A low fence skirted a short flight of stairs leading down to the largest basin, built several feet below street level. They moved towards the front of the fountain with difficulty, their progress impeded by the many tourists crowding close to the water's edge.

"There is something magical about the fountains in Rome," Randy said as they watched the spray of water dancing around and cascading off of the gleaming white sculptures. "The Trevi is the largest baroque fountain in the city."

"It's gigantic," Heather exclaimed. "I've never seen one built into the side of a building before."

Lana could safely say it was one of the most unique fountains she had ever seen. A rocky outcrop carved of Travertine stone was built onto the side of a wide building located in the heart of Rome. The fountain, several stories tall and many feet wide, dwarfed the visitors congregating around its base. From her guidebooks, Lana knew the sculptures told the story of how a young Roman girl showed thirsty soldiers where a hidden spring was, the same source that ultimately became the main water supply for Rome. At the back of the fountain were Corinthian pillars and niches containing statues of the gods Abundance and Health.

In front of them, giant rocks tumbled forward, and water spilled out into tiered basins running down the center. Despite the water constantly flowing over them, the edges of the stones were jagged and sharp. The god Oceanus was visible above the boulders, standing atop a chariot pulled by seahorses that were riding through the powerful spray. The horses' frothy mouths and hooves, frozen in midair, reinforced their exertion and exhaustion.

The sculptures, iconography, and mesmerizing spray were magical. Lana could stay here for hours watching the ever-changing spectacle before her. Unfortunately, most tourists seemed to feel the same way and were elbowing each other for the best positions to take selfies, snap photos, or simply rest while they enjoyed the view. Several security officers walking through the dense crowd kept visitors on their feet and away from the water.

"Wait a second—this is the fountain you can wish to come back to Rome!" Heather exclaimed before shoving her way to the edge of the marble basin. She dug in her purse until she found a coin, then held it up in triumph. "Does anyone know which shoulder you're supposed to throw this over?"

"I thought it was the right one," Bruce said.

"Are you sure? I thought the left one," Katherine said.

Craig made a show of pulling out his phone and typing in their question. "According to the city's website, if you toss a coin with your right hand over your left shoulder and it lands in the water, then you're guaranteed to return to Rome."

"Good enough for me," Heather said as she closed her eyes, then threw it.

Lana wondered whether the coin had even made it into the water. The plethora of tourists crowding the main basin was starting to get on her nerves.

"Are you ready to have a gelato before we head back to the hotel?" Randy asked. "Jake should be arriving in a few hours, and then we'll go to dinner at that café in the Trastevere district."

"Yum, I've been waiting to try the Italian ice cream. Gloria told you about where to go, right?" Katherine asked.

"Yep, it's next to the Pantheon and around the corner from Bernini's elephant carrying an Egyptian obelisk statue. We shouldn't miss it."

"Are you joking about the elephant?" Heather asked.

"Nope. It's one of my favorite statues in Rome, actually. Should we head over now?"

"Sounds good," Heather said. "We're happy to follow your lead."

"Any chance of getting something more substantial to eat along the way? All this walking is sapping my energy," Craig said.

"Sure, we can pick up a few snacks on the way," Randy said.

"What kind of snacks?"

Randy's eyes twinkled. "The Roman kind."

9

An Unexpected Guest

When Jake's taxi arrived at 7 p.m., Randy and the rest were already down in the hotel's lobby waiting for him. Because they only had two hours to eat dinner before the bachelor party was set to begin, Randy wanted to leave for the restaurant as soon as his friend had stashed his bags in his hotel room. He was certain Jake wouldn't mind being rushed despite being jet-lagged; Randy assured everyone that he was always up for anything.

As much as she was looking forward to dinner, Lana was still full from her gelato and the Roman snacks Randy had bought them. The *suppli*, deep-fried balls of rice filled with deliciously stretchy mozzarella, and *trapizzino*, triangle pockets of pizza dough filled with eggplant and cheese, were to die for.

Luckily they'd had a chance to burn some calories by doing a little shopping on the way back. Lana couldn't resist picking up carved wooden Pinocchio puppets for herself and her best friend, Willow. She knew the fairy tale was Italian, but hadn't expected to see so many stores selling the friendly little puppet who became a real boy.

When Jake entered the lobby, Randy jumped up to greet his friend. "Hey, man, glad you could make it."

"I wouldn't have missed this for the world," Jake said as he slapped Randy on the back.

Jake was slightly shorter than Randy, but similar in build. As soon as she saw him, Lana remembered talking to him briefly at Randy's birthday party. She recalled him being incredibly sure of himself, but otherwise seemed alright.

As she watched the two friends interact, Lana realized that while physically they could be brothers, their clothing and personal styling choices were wildly different. Whereas Randy's attire could be best described as grunge, Jake's clothes bore the logos of expensive brands, despite being casual wear, and his eyebrows seemed sculpted. Lana bet he plucked them.

"Hey, everybody! Great to see you all. Nice jackets." He patted his bag. "Don't worry—Randy told me to bring mine, as well."

Jake took his out and pulled it on, winking at Katherine and Heather as he did. "It's like a company get-together, but in Italy."

"I doubt our boss would ever splurge for such an extravagant party," Heather said with a laugh.

"You've got a point there," Katherine agreed.

When the hotel doors opened again, the sound of a bus honking its horn drew Lana's attention to the entrance. A gorgeous, dark-haired woman stepped inside and looked around the lobby, obviously searching for someone. Lana noticed that several men instinctively straightened up their postures and sucked in their bellies. Something about the woman's haughty demeanor made Lana dislike her immediately. She watched as the stranger scanned the crowd, a smile appearing on her face when she homed in on Jake.

When the woman strode towards them, approaching Randy from behind, Jake noticed her, too.

"Oh, yeah—look who I ran into at the airport," he said as he turned and pointed to the stranger.

When Randy turned to see who Jake meant, his expression turned grim. "What's she doing here?"

The rest of the group seemed to freeze, their eyes widening in shock or fear—Lana wasn't certain.

Jake's grin wavered. "What's wrong?"

The woman smiled broadly as she threw her hands up in the air. "Surprise!"

When no one reacted, the woman jutted her chin out at Katherine. "Can't you even say hello? Cat got your tongue again, little sister?"

"Sister?" Lana mumbled. Now that they were standing next to each other, Lana could see the resemblance in their heart-shaped faces and slender build. Yet the new arrival's brightly colored tank top and short skirt contrasted greatly with Katherine's preference for long pants and shirts in subdued shades of brown and gray.

Katherine scowled at the new arrival. "You know I hate that expression, Rachel."

Lana's mouth dropped open. This was Rachel—Randy's stalker and the reason why no one knew exactly where the wedding was taking place? How the heck had she found out about them being in Rome?

When Katherine didn't move, Rachel walked up to her sister and air hugged her. "Great to see you, sis. I didn't know you and Bruce would be here. But then again, we haven't spoken in months. You two are always too busy to make time for me," Rachel said, then pulled back from her sibling. "Don't worry, that will change soon enough."

"Not if I have any say in the matter," Katherine muttered.

"Leave her alone, Rachel," Heather growled.

"Ah, yes, the defender of the meek, to the rescue. What's your latest crusade—whales? Dolphins? I bet it's owls," Rachel tittered.

"You make my blood boil! It should have been you on that ladder, not Randy!" Heather smoldered.

Rachel ignored her remark and, instead, grinned up at Katherine's boyfriend.

Bruce cast his eyes downward as he mumbled a half-hearted hello.

"Where's my hug, Brucie?" Rachel asked as she moved towards him.

"Brucie?" Katherine raged as she glared at her boyfriend.

His face turned a dark shade of crimson as he took a large step backwards, away from Rachel.

"What are you doing here?" Katherine hissed as Rachel wrapped her arms around Bruce's waist anyway.

Lana's eyes bulged out of her head when she observed Rachel's hand moving down towards Bruce's backside. He must have noticed too, because he suddenly sprung out of her embrace and cowered behind Katherine.

"I couldn't miss Randy's wedding," Rachel said as she turned to Randy, smiling warmly at him.

"You can't be within three hundred feet of either me or Gloria!" he growled.

Lana had never seen him so upset before and was rather frightened by the force of his anger.

Rachel looked slightly perturbed by his reaction, but not at all frightened. "The restraining order is for Washington state, not Europe. I checked."

Jake stepped in between Rachel and Randy. "A restraining order? I didn't know you two knew each other that well."

"Randy and I go way back, don't we?" She leaned around Jake to try to touch Randy's arm, but he swatted her hand away.

Unfazed by Randy's rejection, Rachel turned to the rest. "So gang, what are we doing today? Tossing coins into Trevi Fountain? Visiting the Vatican? Have you had a gelato yet? I could use two scoops right about now."

Lana remained silent, stunned by the differences in Randy and Rachel's reactions. It was as if Rachel was completely unaware of the discomfort and pain she was causing Randy.

"Stay away from me and my friends!" he bellowed, startling pretty much everyone in the lobby. Several hotel guests and staff members had been watching the fight play out from a distance, but Randy's last outburst motivated two security guards to move closer towards the group.

Rachel laughed off Randy's remark. "Technically, your friends are my family members and colleagues, which means I have every right to stay."

"They aren't your coworkers anymore!" Randy raged.

Rachel cocked her head. "Didn't you hear? I'm going to be working for Straight Up again—starting next month. That's how Jake and I know each other; we met when I came in to fill out the paperwork."

Randy turned to his friends, despair and anger clouding his expression. "Why didn't you tell me? How could our boss hire her again, after what she did to me?"

Katherine paled as she began to tremble. "Our boss wouldn't do that to me, either. Would he?"

"After what she did to Randy, how could they hire her again?" Heather cried.

"Because I did nothing wrong," Rachel huffed. "Hello? I'm standing right here. Jeez, what is wrong with you people?"

"I'm going to call our boss as soon as we get home and get to the bottom of this. I'll quit Straight Up if it's true, Randy," Heather insisted.

"You little hussy—you slept with one of the managers, didn't you?" Randy asserted.

Rachel's slap across his face rang through the lobby. "How dare you! If it wasn't for your lies and accusations, they wouldn't have forced me to take a season off. I didn't cause your accident, and I have every right to work there."

Randy held his reddening cheek with one hand as he pointed to the door with the other. "Stay away from me. Get out of this hotel and leave me alone!"

Rachel folded her hands over her torso. "Make me."

A primal scream filled the room as Randy lunged towards Rachel, pushing her so hard that she fell backwards against one of the many stone pillars dotting the expansive lobby. As she slid down to the ground, Rachel's head left a smear of blood on one.

Lana stood frozen in place, shocked to see her fellow guide violently shove a woman. She'd never seen Randy lift a finger to anyone before.

"What did you do?" Craig raged as he and Jake ran to Rachel's aid.

Randy stared at his hands as if they belonged to someone else. Two of the hotel's security guards closed in but stopped short of tackling him, instead standing as if they were ready to block off his escape.

"I didn't know you liked to play rough, Randy," Rachel cackled. "There's so much we don't know about each other yet."

"And never will. I want you out of my life, permanently. What do I have to do to make you leave me alone?"

After Craig and Jake helped her to her feet, Rachel shook her arms loose and strode over to Randy. "As long as there is breath in my body, you can bet I'll be keeping tabs on you. We're soul mates, Randy, and one day you'll realize that, too."

"Gloria is the one I want to be with, not you. That's what bothers you so much, isn't it? That I don't want to be with you. I was tired of your manipulative mind games then, just as I am now."

"Gloria has brainwashed you. Would you feel the same way if she was out of the picture?"

Randy shoved his face into hers. "Don't you go near her!"

"I can do whatever I want—this is a free country." Rachel turned to the rest. "Say, where is the wedding taking place, anyway?"

"Don't you say a word!" Randy threatened.

"Calm down, we don't even know where it is, remember? You didn't trust any of us enough to tell us," Craig said as he took Randy's arm and began pulling him away. "Why don't you take a walk and cool down?"

Katherine stepped in front of Craig and glared at her sister. "No. Randy shouldn't have to go—this is his party. Rachel, why can't you leave us be? Randy has made it abundantly clear that he doesn't want to be with you. Move on."

Lana's eyebrows shot up. Considering Katherine's wallflower-like demeanor, she hadn't expected her to stand up for Randy or admonish Rachel. They were sisters, after all.

"I flew all the way over here so I could congratulate the bride in person. Besides, I want to see Gloria's wedding dress. I hope it's not white; that would be hypocritical. I'm not leaving you alone until I know where the wedding is being held."

Lana was glad that Craig was holding Randy back; he looked as if he could strangle Rachel with his bare hands.

"If you know what's good for you, you'll leave me and Gloria alone—or else," Randy snarled.

"Or else what? You couldn't hurt little ole me. Deep down you know we are meant to be together."

"What is wrong with you?" Katherine cried as she pointed to the door. "Get out of here! We don't want you here."

Rachel turned to Bruce, who immediately looked to the floor.

When she made eye contact with Jake, he shrugged and nodded to the hotel's entrance. "I'll catch up with you later," he mumbled.

"I can tell when I'm not welcome," Rachel said. "I'm going to check into my hotel now, but don't worry, Randy. It's close by so I'll be able to keep an eye on you." She laughed as she picked up her bag and sauntered out of the lobby.

Randy glared at Rachel's retreating figure. "What did I ever do to deserve having that psychopath in my life?"

He looked to Katherine. "Sorry, I know she's your sister."

Katherine laid a hand on his arm. "It's okay. She's been trouble since birth. You're the only man who has had the audacity to leave her. That's why she's obsessed with you. If only she could find a lover as twisted as she is, then she might leave you alone."

Randy nodded before turning to the rest. "How did Rachel find out about the wedding? Has anyone had contact with her recently and let it slip?"

"Of course not!" Heather exclaimed. "We all know how much she hurt you."

"Sorry, you're right. Rachel being here is doing my head in. I have to call Gloria. She's terrified of Rachel and I don't know how she's going to react to this news."

Randy looked to Bruce. "I really appreciate you arranging my bachelor party, but Rachel's presence changes everything."

"Come on," Jake said. "Now that Rachel has had her fun, she'll leave you alone. Right?"

"I can't take that chance. Gloria means everything to me. I am not going to be able to enjoy the bachelor party tonight, knowing Rachel is in the same country as my fiancée."

10

It Was No Accident

When Randy rushed off towards the staircase leading up to their rooms, Lana ran over and grabbed his arm. When he turned on her, the wild look in his eyes made her release her grip immediately.

"Randy, stop. You're scaring me. What happened between you and Rachel to make you act so crazy?"

He ran a hand through his wavy red hair as he let out a sigh. "I can't believe I lost control so easily, but she gets right under my skin. Rachel has caused me so much pain, I will not let her hurt Gloria."

"But why would she want to harm your fiancée?"

"Because she's bonkers—that's why!"

Lana's puzzled expression caused his fierce expression to soften. He nodded towards the top of the staircase. "Walk with me."

Lana did her best to keep up as Randy took the steps two at a time.

"After I broke up with Rachel, she started stalking me. At first, I thought it was coincidence that I ran into her at REI or the organic market, but I soon realized that she was following me. When I confronted her about it, she laughed and said she could do whatever she wanted. We still worked together, which made it incredibly difficult to avoid her completely. Though Katherine did her best to schedule us on different days."

"That's horrible, Randy. I had no idea."

"Things really worsened after I met Gloria. She started working at Straight

Up Climbs a few weeks after I broke up with Rachel, and I fell for her real hard. Rachel saw us leaving work together and followed us on some of our dates. She'd wave or call out my name, but I ignored her, and Gloria didn't seem to notice. Until I took Gloria to the Seattle Space Needle for our two-month anniversary. Rachel showed up and ruined it."

"What did she do exactly?"

"She had the waiter bring over a drink, from my wife, he said. Then she walked over to our table and French-kissed me, right in front of Gloria! And when I protested, she called Gloria a horrible name and stormed off."

"No way! What did you do?" Lana panted as she rushed to keep up. *That explains why Gloria quit working at Straight Up Climbs*, she thought.

"It took a lot of explaining to keep Gloria from walking away. I'd already told her that I'd recently broken up with a coworker, but Rachel's actions made her think I was lying to her. After Katherine reassured her that I was telling the truth, and not Rachel, she finally started taking my calls again. She quit working for Straight Up Climbs, but did stick with me and put up with Rachel's irritating behavior. At least, until Rachel sent a black rose to her house with a note that said if she didn't leave me be, the next time it would be lilies."

Lana stopped on the staircase, staring up at her friend. "That is insane."

"You can say that again. It freaked Gloria out so much that she stayed with her parents for a few weeks. I went to Rachel's house and told her if she didn't leave us alone, I'd go to the police. But she didn't take me seriously. Instead, she kept insisting that Gloria was all wrong for me. Nothing I said got through to her; she refused to accept that I didn't want to be with her. I felt like I had no choice but to take legal action."

"Oh, Randy, what a nightmare." Lana felt so bad that she didn't know about his past. He was always so upbeat and carefree, she'd never have guessed that he'd dealt with a stalker.

"It got worse. The day after I threatened her, my ladder's safety catch broke while I was climbing over a deep crevasse. Luckily, it snapped as soon as I put my full weight on it, so my partner was able to arrest my fall and prevent me from landing on the bottom of the fissure. But when the ladder crashed against the ice, it crushed my leg and shattered several bones. That's why I had to look for a new job."

Lana paused midstep, trying to understand his train of thought. His friends had already told her their theories about his accident, but she was most curious to know what Randy believed to be true. "That's horrible, but why do you think Rachel was responsible for your accident?"

"It was no accident. The clasp let loose as soon as I stepped onto the second rung. That doesn't just happen. Rachel must have bent it enough to hold while I was placing the ladder, but not enough to carry my weight. The police couldn't prove it, which is why it's officially an accident. But my boss was so concerned about Rachel's possible involvement that he grounded her. I thought permanently, but apparently it was only for one season."

Lana considered his words. "Even if someone did weaken the safety latch, why do you think Rachel tampered with your gear? Isn't Heather responsible for the equipment?"

"Because of the timing. Rachel was supposed to place that ladder, but she suddenly came down with food poisoning, so I had to take her place at the last minute. She'd already gotten the gear from Heather and could have easily bent the clasp with a tang. Rachel had never been sick at work before; it must have been a lie to get me out on that ladder."

When Lana remained silent, Randy pulled on his hair. "It was a setup—she sabotaged the ladder intentionally so that it would collapse, but in a way that would have been impossible to find afterwards. Don't you see? Rachel was convinced we were meant to be together. If she couldn't have me, then no one could."

Lana cocked her head at her friend. "You know I think you're a great guy, but I still don't understand why Rachel is so obsessed with you."

"Because I dared to dump her. Rachel is incredibly manipulative and controlling. She refused to accept that our relationship was over. Considering her behavior tonight, she still can't accept it. I can't believe she showed up here! I have to go to Gloria. After that fall, I was so full of rage and frustration. Yet Gloria stuck by my side through it all. When I was able to walk again, she was the one who encouraged me to apply at Wanderlust Tours. It's thanks to her that I'm not stuck in a rut and drinking my life away. She really is the best thing that's ever happened to me, and I'm not going to let that psychopath hurt her."

Lana pulled her friend in for a hug. "You do whatever you need to do. I'll take care of your friends. Please let me know what Gloria says, and send her my love."

11

Paranoia

"Where's Randy?" Heather asked as she looked around Lana and up the empty staircase.

"He's checking in with Gloria. Since he might be a while, he said we should go to dinner as planned. He'll join us as soon as he can." Lana hated lying to his friends, but Randy needed time to deal with this Rachel situation.

Heather folded her arms over her torso. "I would rather wait for Randy. He might need our help."

"If we do, we probably won't have time for a full meal," Lana counseled. "Let's give him space to talk with Gloria. He's pretty upset about Rachel showing up and needs to talk to his fiancée about what he's feeling."

"Craig and I are here—he could talk to one of us," Heather pouted.

Heather is definitely having trouble letting Randy go, Lana thought. Why was she unable to accept that Randy had a new best friend—one he wanted to marry? It was as if Heather refused to see that he was moving on with his life. Yet Lana still didn't see the romantic infatuation that Craig did. To her, seemed as if Heather was used to being the one Randy relied on and confided in, and she wasn't ready to give up her place in his inner circle.

"I'm ready to go to dinner now," Jake said.

"Do you mind if I take a minute to freshen up before we head over?" Katherine asked.

"That's a great idea," Lana said. "I'm going to do the same. Can we meet back here in fifteen minutes?" Popping back up to her room would give her time to check on Randy without the others wondering what she was up to.

"Do you want to join me?" Katherine asked her boyfriend.

"Sure," Bruce said as he leaned in to peck her cheek.

Katherine blushed, clearly reveling in the affection.

Jake stood up and looked around until he spotted a reading table at the back of the lobby, its surface covered in magazines and newspapers in several languages. "I'm going to wait over there," he said.

"There's a church I want to see before we have dinner. It's close to the restaurant. Anyone want to visit it with me?" Craig asked.

"No thanks. A good meal sounds better than sightseeing right now," Bruce said, garnering nods from the rest.

"Okay, well, I'll see you at the café," Craig said and headed towards the lobby door.

"Have fun. We'll see you soon," Lana said.

"I'm going to grab a mineral water from the hotel bar and meet you back here in a few minutes," Heather said, and Lana smiled in acknowledgment.

Bruce took his girlfriend's arm and guided her towards the stairs.

"See you in a minute, Jake," Lana called out and trailed after them.

When Katherine walked past the lobby door, her head turned sharply and her lips puckered down, as if she'd spotted something disagreeable. Lana's guard went up. Was Rachel lurking outside? Lana followed Katherine's gaze but didn't see anyone familiar.

The three of them continued upstairs. Luckily, their rooms were on different floors. When she returned to hers, Randy was standing outside her door.

"What did Gloria say?" Lana asked after she'd let him into her room.

"She is terrified, which is not how you are supposed to feel right before you get married. At least, not for this reason. She and her parents want me to come to the vineyard right away. Lana, they are talking about forbidding my friends from attending, for fear that Rachel will follow them. They don't even want Alex to come!"

Randy looked so distraught. She knew how important it was to both brothers that Alex be present at Randy's wedding.

"I'm so sorry. It's horrible to have to make that drastic decision, but if Gloria's family is worried about your safety, then we won't come to the wedding. Period."

Randy cast his droopy dog eyes to the floor. "That isn't how I want to get married. I invited you all over here because I want to share this moment with you. Let me get to the village so I can talk with them face to face, before we decide how to proceed."

Lana's heart went out to him. "I feel terrible for you and Gloria. If there is anything I can do for you..."

"Keeping everyone occupied tonight would be great."

"I'm already on it. We're going to walk over to the restaurant in a few minutes, and I've told them that you hope to join us later."

"That's perfect. I'm going to go to the train station and change my ticket. Please don't tell my friends that I've left until after dinner. That should give me enough time to get out of the city. I don't know how Rachel found out about the wedding, but one of them must have told her."

Poor Randy, Lana thought, *he is so upset that he is becoming paranoid.* "I promise not to say anything. Do what you need to do to care of your fiancée. I'll keep the rest busy."

"Great," Randy said, but Lana could tell he wasn't really listening. His thoughts were already traveling to Florence and then to Gloria's village beyond—somewhere in Tuscany.

"Thanks, Lana. You're a lifesaver." He gave her a quick hug, then fled the room.

Lana hoped he wasn't being literal.

12

A Chase Through Rome

Lana touched up her makeup before pulling on her Straight Up jacket and grabbing her purse. When she switched off her bedroom light, intending to leave and round up Randy's friends, the pinkish glow of the setting sun drew her to the window. The streaks of oranges and purple lit up the sky dramatically behind the tiled roofs of the Roman skyline. It was quite a glorious sight to see.

Lana sighed, wishing again that Alex were here with her. As she turned towards her hotel room door, two women engaged in an argument down on the sidewalk caught her attention. The woman facing her was Katherine, Lana quickly realized. She squinted against the setting sun to better see the other person. It was Rachel!

What the heck is she doing down there? Lana wondered. Had Rachel been outside waiting for Randy this whole time? Or had her sister asked her to come back to their hotel?

Whatever it was they were discussing, their body language made clear that it was not a pleasant conversation. Lana opened her window to try to hear what they were arguing about, but their voices were drowned out by the traffic noise. The quarrel intensified when Rachel jabbed a finger into Katherine's chest. Lana figured Katherine would back down, but instead she slapped her sister hard, sending Rachel's head reeling backwards.

"You will pay for that!" Rachel yelled, loud enough for everyone in the street to hear.

"If you don't leave me and Bruce alone, you'll be the one who pays, dear sister!" Katherine screeched before storming back inside the hotel.

Rachel started to follow, but quickly stopped and retreated into the shadows created by the setting sun.

Lana went to close the window, figuring the show was over, when she noticed Randy exiting the hotel. Her heart began to pound when she noted how dangerously close his path was to Rachel's current position.

However, Randy was walking at a clipped pace while talking on the phone and seemed oblivious to her presence. Moments after he passed Rachel, she stepped out behind him, matching his stride.

Oh, no! Lana thought. This was exactly what Randy was afraid might happen—that Rachel would follow one of them to the train station and discover the location of Gloria's village.

Lana leaned out the window and screamed to her friend, "Randy—look behind you!"

However, the street noise must have muffled her voice because neither Rachel nor Randy reacted.

Lana grabbed her phone and dialed his number, but he didn't answer. "Rachel is following you, Randy! Be careful," she spoke into his voicemail, making her tone as urgent as possible.

After a moment's indecision, Lana skipped down the stairs and burst through the front doors, racing to catch up with her friend and his stalker. She had to warn Randy that Rachel was tailing him before he made it to the station. The last thing anyone wanted was for Rachel to find out which train he was going to take. If she somehow boarded it and confronted Randy, Lana was afraid he might throw Rachel off of it.

When she arrived at the main street, she scanned both sides but didn't see Randy or Rachel. The sidewalks were far less busy than during the day, and only a handful of tourists were walking around.

The changing weather was probably encouraging visitors to stay indoors, Lana thought, as tiny drops of rain splattered onto her jacket. She looked up to see the previously clear skies were quickly filling with angry, dark clouds.

She pulled her jacket collar tighter around her neck and jogged along the pavement towards the Tiber River, hoping Randy was walking to the train station instead of catching a cab. As she approached the river's edge, Lana spotted Rachel crossing the Ponte Cavour, a wide bridge connecting the Prati neighborhood to the city's center.

"Rachel! Stop!" Lana screamed, but her prey didn't break stride. Instead, Rachel continued sprinting over the bridge before turning right.

Lana ran to catch up, but by the time she'd crossed the Tiber River, she'd lost sight of her. And there were three streets leading off to the right. Lana chose the last option, running down the Via di Ripetta while frantically searching the crowds for any sign of Randy or Rachel. As she passed the Palazzo Borghese, she spotted a Straight Up jacket in the distance.

"Wait up, Randy!" she screamed, but the long sprint had taken the force out of her voice. When she began to jog towards him, the person glanced backwards. Yet he didn't stop and wait for her, instead tearing off down a side street. When he turned the corner, Lana saw the person clearly in profile. It wasn't Randy.

"Jake?" she called out, unsure whether her eyes were deceiving her. She bent over to catch her breath, before charging onward.

When she reached the next intersection, Lana scanned the crossroads for the person in the jacket. She didn't see him anywhere.

"Drat!" Lana fumed aloud before quickly consulting her map. The train station was on the other side of town. Because of the mazelike structure of the inner city, it was easier to navigate by landmarks than roads. Lana chose Trevi Fountain as her next destination. As she folded up her map, the skies opened up, and a sheet of cold rain poured down on her.

"Great," Lana mumbled as she set off through the heart of Rome's expansive city center. The rain didn't let up but seemed to increase in intensity, to the point that she could barely see her hand in front of her face. Motivated by the increasing downpour, Lana ran towards her destination, keeping the signs pointing towards the fountain in sight as she did.

When she heard the sound of rushing water, Lana knew she was getting close. Thanks to the bright spotlights shining on the statues and pools of water, the Trevi Fountain was even more majestic than it had been in the morning, even through the sheets of rain pouring down from the skies.

Lana ducked under an awning and shook off her clothes before she consulted her map again, searching for the next landmark. When she looked up to orient herself, Heather jogged past, but didn't seem to notice her. The rain was streaming off of her Straight Up jacket, yet she made no effort to shield her head.

"Heather?" Lana called out. The girl turned towards her voice, but as soon as they made eye contact, the younger woman darted away. Lana shoved her map into her pocket and ran to catch up, but Heather was already out of sight.

What the heck is going on? Lana wondered. Why were Jake and Heather following Randy, as well?

Lana pulled out her phone and dialed Randy's number. Again, her call went to voicemail. "Randy, I lost Rachel, but I know she is following you. If she tries to confront you, walk away. She's not worth it. Be careful, buddy!"

She felt powerless, but there was nothing more she could do to help him. Was Rachel following Randy in order to discover his wedding's location? Or did she want to try to convince him they should be together? And if he refused to listen, would she harm him? Or would Randy lash out again?

Lana continued on to the train station as a fountain of questions rumbled through her mind. Despite the stillness of the streets, the station was incredibly busy. The whistles of conductors announcing trains' departures echoed through the vast hall as tourists of all nationalities crossed her path.

After walking past the multitude of ticket machines dotted around the massive station, Lana made her way to the platform where trains to Florence arrived and departed, but didn't see her fellow guide. It looked like there were several trains traveling between the two cities each hour. Maybe Randy had already left, she thought. The only light point of the night was that during her wanderings around the station, Lana had not seen Rachel. *Maybe she gave up*, Lana hoped.

Unsure as to what else she could do, Lana decided to return to the hotel. She retraced her steps, using the signs for the Trevi Fountain as her guide.

This time, however, her approach was hindered by a strand of police tape.

"What now?" she muttered.

An ambulance was parked in the middle of Piazza di Trevi, effectively blocking off the staircase leading down to the basin's edge. A row of officers pointed her towards the street running along one side of the fountain. Lana did as they asked and slowly walked away, pausing at the fence to better watch the macabre scene unfolding before her.

Through the decorative fence, she could see that several paramedics and policemen had waded into the main basin. They were bent over, as if they were trying to pick something up out of the water. Lana's stomach tightened when she noticed a cloud of red flowed and ebbed around their legs.

Whatever they were tugging on soon came loose, and then they were guiding it towards the pool's edge. Lana sucked in her breath when she noticed that it was a pair of legs they were holding onto. The person's torso and head were still out of her view, blocked by the jagged rocks filling the fountain's basin.

As the officers slowly moved the body to the open water, a medic stopped their progress and gently turned the corpse over. When they did, the victim's long dark hair cascaded over her lifeless face. As the strands parted, Lana felt a scream race out of her throat as she grabbed onto the railing for support.

"Rachel!"

13

Police Escort

Lana pulled her jacket tight around her shoulders, trying in vain to shield her skin from the cold evening breeze. The investigating officer had questioned her for more than an hour about her connection to Rachel, yet still seemed unsatisfied with her answers.

She understood his frustration. Lana couldn't tell him Rachel's last name, where she was staying in Rome, or why she wanted to disrupt Randy's wedding. It didn't help that some of her explanations were intentionally vague. Until she knew what had happened between Rachel and Randy on the way to the train station, she didn't want to cast her friend's actions in a bad light.

After a brief pause to confer with the policemen still combing the scene, the officer was back again to ask her the same questions.

"Ms. Hansen, you claim the victim, who you only know as Rachel, was in Rome to interrupt Randy Wright's wedding. Can you further enlighten me?" The officer paused dramatically and cocked an eyebrow at her.

"I wish I could, but I cannot. As I already told you, I only met her a few hours ago. She surprised our group when we were down in the hotel lobby. And I'd never heard Randy mention her before. I can tell you what her last name is as soon as I check our itinerary, which is back at the hotel. I assume she and her sister, Katherine, share the same family name. "

Lana paused a moment as her mind registered what had been bothering her about the officer's questions. "Why don't you know what Rachel's last name is? Didn't she have a wallet or purse with her?"

"No, she did not, and my colleagues did not find anything stuck in the fountain's drains. Which leads us to believe that this was not an accident, but a robbery gone wrong."

"Then it couldn't have been my friend. Randy wouldn't have robbed her."

"He would have, if he wished to cast suspicion on a stranger."

Lana pursed her lips. "I suppose…"

"Can your friends tell me more about Rachel's intentions?"

"They aren't really my friends, but friends of Randy. We all flew in to attend his wedding on December 24."

"Christmas Eve is an unusual time to marry."

"I don't know, I think it's pretty romantic. Look, Rachel's sister is one of those friends. Don't you think someone should let her know that Rachel is dead?"

"I would prefer to tell her myself, in person. Where do you think Randy's friends are right now?"

Lana looked to her watch. "It's almost ten o'clock. I bet they are done with dinner. The men had plans to go to a gladiator school, but I doubt they'll attend." As soon as the words exited her mouth, Lana knew she'd made a mistake.

"Why not?"

"It was part of Randy's bachelor party, which he canceled at the last minute because Rachel showed up."

"And where is Randy now?"

"On a train to Florence, as far as I know. His fiancée is already at her family home in Tuscany, and he is joining her so he can help get everything ready for the wedding."

"Which village is that?"

"I don't know," Lana mumbled.

The officer startled at her answer. "Do you not know the name of the village your friend is getting married in, or is it difficult for you to pronounce? You can write it down for me, if you prefer."

The officer held out his pen and notepad.

"No, I don't know where it is or what it's called. It is supposed to be a surprise," Lana said, knowing her answer made no sense.

"Why would the name of the village be a surprise?" he pushed.

"I don't know—it just is," she said resolutely.

"Why don't you write down Randy's phone number, then call his friends and ask them to return to their hotel. I wish to speak to all of them. It is important to find out when they saw Rachel last."

Lana jotted down Randy's number, then dialed Heather's phone. When she started to walk away, the officer cleared his throat and crooked his finger, beckoning her back.

"Put the call on speaker phone," he demanded.

Lana did as she was told. When Heather answered, they could hear dance music blaring in the background.

"Hey, Lana. Where are you? We just found the most fabulous bar," Heather shouted into the receiver.

"Good to know. I wasn't certain whether you were still at the café," Lana yelled back.

"We finished dinner a half hour ago, and since the gladiator school isn't happening, we decided to get a drink instead. Do you want to join us? I can give you the address."

"I'm afraid I'm going to have to ask you all to come back to the hotel. There's been an accident, and the police need to speak to us all."

"Is it Randy or Gloria?" Heather shrieked.

"They are alright. It's—"

The policeman grabbed at Lana's phone.

She wrestled it back from him long enough to add, "I need to go, but can you all go back to the hotel now? The police will be there any minute."

"Okay," Heather replied just as the officer succeeded in grabbing Lana's phone and ending the call.

"Why did you do that? Why can't I tell her what happened?"

"Because I wish to see their reactions when they find out Rachel is dead. Shall we? You can ride with me in the patrol car."

14

Expressions of Grief

Randy's friends entered the hotel lobby, laughing and carefree. At least, until they spotted Lana and the pair of police officers waiting for them by the reception desk. That sobered them right up.

After everyone had shuffled into an empty conference room at the back of the hotel, the lead investigator introduced himself and his colleague, before asking to see their passports.

"What happened? Why are you here?" Heather demanded. "Is Randy alright?"

The investigator ignored the urgency in her voice. "After I know who you are, I will explain why I am here."

The two policemen jotted down their names and passport numbers, confirming visually who was who before returning them. The only passport that seemed to give the officers pause was Katherine's. Lana assumed it was because she had already told them that she was Rachel's sister. When one policeman showed Katherine's document to the other, they stepped away from the table to confer privately before giving hers back. Once finished, the lead officer folded his hands onto the table and took in the group before him.

"I regret to inform you that Rachel Merriweather is dead. Her body was found in the Trevi Fountain earlier this evening."

Heather gasped loudly as Randy's friends looked to Katherine. Lana did, too, expecting to see a flood of tears streaming down her face or passionate cries of denial. Yet, other than blinking slightly more rapidly than normal, Katherine's expression and demeanor didn't change one bit.

Lana was shocked by her lack of emotion. It was obvious from their interactions that the sisters weren't close, yet she would have expected Katherine to care that her sibling had drowned. Had the officer's words not gotten through? Perhaps Katherine needed more time to process this horrible news before she could react to it.

"How can that be?" Bruce asked. His voice was choked with emotion as he wiped the tears from his cheeks. He seemed more distraught by Rachel's death than Katherine was.

However, his reaction was nothing compared to Jake's. "I can't believe that she's really gone," he moaned before breaking down into choking sobs.

"It appears she had sustained multiple head injuries, but our medical team suspects the cause of death was drowning. We have to complete the autopsy before we can be certain."

Jake's cries intensified, and Craig looked as if he was going to be sick.

The investigator looked to Katherine, his tone gentle. "I understand she was your sister. I am sorry for your loss."

"Yes, she was. Thank you," Katherine said as she shifted slightly in her seat. Her tone was incredibly formal and distant.

He observed her for a moment before asking, "Why is your sister staying in another hotel?"

"Bruce and I flew in this morning, but neither of us knew Rachel was coming. I assume she didn't tell me because she knew I would disapprove."

The officer's brow crinkled. "Why would you disapprove of her flying to Rome?"

"This isn't an ordinary vacation. We are all here to attend our friend Randy's wedding. Rachel is Randy's ex, so she is the last person I would have expected to see here. But I should have known she would try to ruin the wedding for him. They'd dated briefly, and she refused to accept that he broke up with her. She was quite obsessive, my sister, and very selfish." Katherine spat the words out. "She couldn't stand that Randy left her, that silly cow."

How could Katherine speak so poorly of her recently deceased sister—especially in front of the police, Lana wondered. It was akin to putting an "arrest me—I did it!" T-shirt on.

The officer, on the other hand, seemed unfazed by Katherine's outburst. Lana reckoned that in his line of work, he had witnessed many expressions of grief. "Did you fight with Rachel about her actions?"

"No, I did not." Katherine raised her chin up in the air. "After she showed up at the hotel and made a scene, I told her to leave us alone. She did leave shortly after—so she could check into her hotel, she said. But I don't know where she was staying and I didn't see her after that."

Lana's eyebrows knitted together. That wasn't right. She had seen Katherine and Rachel fighting outside this hotel right before Randy left for the train station. Why would Katherine lie?

"What do you mean—made a scene?"

"She surprised us down in the lobby a few hours ago. Randy wasn't pleased to see her. Frankly, neither was I."

The investigator leaned forward, trying in vain to make eye contact with Katherine. "Did Randy and Rachel argue about her being in Rome?"

Katherine pursed her lips, yet remained silent.

"Yeah, you could say that," Jake responded instead, garnering a nasty look from the rest. His sobs had lessened to sniffles the longer the officer spoke. By now, his cheeks were free from tears.

"What? There's no point in lying—the whole hotel saw them fighting. Randy was raging mad that Rachel had followed him to Italy and blamed one of us for telling her where the wedding was being held." Jake crossed one leg over the other and leaned back. "It wasn't me, but I can't vouch for the rest."

"Just how mad did Randy get?"

"Rachel taunted Randy so badly that he pushed her into one of those pillars in the lobby and she cut her head open."

The officer's eyebrows shot up as he scribbled down the information.

"That was simply bad luck—I bet Randy didn't even push her that hard," Katherine said. "Rachel deserved what she got."

Lana shook her head in confusion. The two sisters must have had a horrible relationship.

The officer let Katherine's comment slide and turned his attention to Jake. "You became quite emotional when I informed everyone of Rachel's death. Were you in a relationship with the deceased?"

The room grew quiet as everyone waited for Jake to respond. "Relationship is a strong word. We met a month ago and had gone out on a few dates," he said, not entirely answering the officer's question.

Craig straightened up and stared at Jake, an evil look in his eye.

His glare also caught the inspector's attention. "Were you also in a relationship with the deceased?"

Craig's expression softened. "No, we weren't together. I had met her a few times when she and Randy were dating, but I hadn't seen her since they broke up."

The officer noted Craig's response, then returned his gaze to Jake. "Do you know if Rachel was seeing anyone else?"

Jake shrugged. "I never asked her to be monogamous."

"I didn't realize you had to ask that of your partner," Craig snarled.

"We hadn't talked about moving in together or anything like that, but I did consider us a couple." He blushed before adding, "But I suspect I was more interested in her than she was in me."

"That's usually how Rachel operated. It gave her a sense of control over the relationship. Randy was the unlucky exception," Katherine butted in, seemingly in Jake's defense.

"What do you mean?" the officer asked.

"Randy was the only one who dared to leave her."

The officer made a notation then looked to Bruce, Craig, and Jake. "Lana Hansen mentioned that you were scheduled to take part in a gladiator school training tonight, but Randy decided to leave Rome instead. Do you know why he left so suddenly?"

Bruce scratched at his ear. "He said that he was worried about Rachel being in town, but he didn't say that he was leaving right away. When he didn't show up at dinner, I tried calling him, but he didn't answer."

"Me, too," Heather added. "Tonight was his bachelor party, and it's not like him to skip something so important without saying something first."

Lana cleared her throat. "I was going to tell you all at dinner that Randy had decided to travel to Florence tonight instead of tomorrow. After he called Gloria, he went straight to the train station."

"Why did you know that he was leaving, but not the others?" the investigator asked.

Lana shifted uncomfortably in her seat. "Because he was worried one of them might tell Rachel where he was going. He didn't want her to know where the wedding was taking place and was concerned she might follow him to the train station."

"It would have been nice to know that earlier—I've been worried sick about him. You could have sent us a message," Heather fumed.

Lana started to retort when the officer said, "She was being questioned by the police so she wasn't able to respond sooner."

"Why were you being questioned?" Heather asked. "Did you hurt Rachel?"

"No! I was walking by Trevi Fountain when her body was discovered," Lana explained.

"That was good luck for us. If she hadn't recognized Rachel, we wouldn't have found you so quickly. Rachel's wallet had been stolen," the officer added.

The rest glared at Lana, making clear they were not grateful for the coincidence.

"Let's go back to the fight between Rachel and Randy. After Rachel left, what did you do? When was the last time any of you saw or spoke to her?"

Randy's friends searched each other's faces, as if looking for the correct answer.

"As I said before, I didn't see her after she left the hotel," Katherine said. Jake and Craig nodded in agreement.

"Me, either," Bruce said. "Katherine and I rested in our room a while before dinner and didn't see anyone else until we walked over to the Trastevere district."

Katherine startled slightly, but the officers didn't seem to notice.

Why was Bruce covering for Katherine by lying about their movements?

Was he trying to protect her because he knew about her fight with Rachel? That did seem to be his role in their relationship. Although Katherine's surprised reaction made Lana wonder whether there wasn't another answer. Perhaps Bruce had also been out of the room and was hoping Katherine would now cover for him.

The investigator wrote down Bruce's statement, then turned his attention to Heather. "Did you see Rachel after this fight in the hotel lobby?"

"No, I did not. I went up to my room to rest, too." Heather's eyes flittered across the group, as if she was daring someone to contradict her.

Lana deliberated telling the officers that she thought she'd seen both Jake and Heather while she was chasing after Randy. Yet, considering she wasn't entirely certain that it really had been them, she decided to keep her mouth shut. The last thing she wanted to do was get one of them into unnecessary trouble. She'd already done enough by leading the police to their group.

"Do any of you know who might have wanted to harm Rachel?"

"None of us did, that's for sure. And I mean Randy, too," Heather insisted. "Rachel was selfish, mean, and man-hungry, but none of us hated her enough to kill her."

"We'll see," the officer said and snapped his notebook shut. "We will soon question Randy Wright about his relationship with Rachel and their recent argument. My team is also gathering video footage from local businesses. We hope to find out more about Rachel's movements so we can better determine if her fall was an accident or murder."

Lana gulped automatically, fearing for Randy's freedom once the police found out about the restraining order he'd obtained against Rachel. Her showing up in Rome with the intention of sabotaging his wedding, as well as her threats against Gloria—made in front of a crowded lobby nonetheless—were excellent reasons for Randy to want Rachel dead.

If only she hadn't identified Rachel, the police never would have tied her to this group. Lana cursed her bad luck. After the officers left, she would have to call Randy and find out more about his walk to the train station.

15

No One Deserves To Die

"Randy! I'm glad I caught you. How are you holding up?" Lana said.

The two policemen were walking out of the hotel when she dialed his number, yet she wasn't certain whether the investigating officer had already ordered that Randy be pulled off the train and brought back to Rome. Once he was in their custody, she figured it would be difficult for him to talk freely.

"Hey, Lana. Sorry I didn't get back to you earlier, but thanks for watching my back and letting me know about Rachel," he said, sounding like his usual self and not at all distraught.

"I'm on the train now, and I didn't see anyone who resembled her getting on it, so I'm feeling much more relaxed. Are my friends mad at me for not telling them that I was leaving early?"

No wonder he sounds normal, the police haven't gotten in touch with him yet, she realized. "No, your friends aren't mad at you. Randy, are you sitting down?"

"I'm on a train, so yes. What's going on, Lana? You sound upset."

"Rachel is dead. The police found her body in Trevi Fountain a few hours ago."

"Are you serious?" His voice choked up with emotion as he began to softly weep. "I hated her for stalking me, but no one deserves to die. What happened?"

"The police don't know for certain yet, but it appears to be a robbery that turned violent. They just finished interviewing me and your friends in an attempt to find out what Rachel was doing in Rome, and if any of us saw anything unusual tonight. They also want to talk to you, so I gave them your contact information."

"Of course, anything they need. Do you think she suffered much?"

Lana's heart went out to him. The woman had made his life a nightmare, and yet he still cared about her as a human being. Randy truly was one in a million.

"The police suspect that she hit her head before she fell into the water. If she was unconscious when she went in, she wouldn't have felt any pain."

Randy whimpered. "She must have been following me when she was attacked! I wish I'd been more aware of my surroundings during that walk. Maybe I would have seen who hurt her. But I was so focused on getting to the station that I wasn't paying attention to what was happening around me. I didn't even notice you'd left those voicemails until after I boarded the train."

"Do you remember what streets you took or monuments you passed? I lost you right before I reached the Trevi, but it had started to rain pretty heavily." Lana prayed he had chosen another path and had proof to back it up. That would make the police interrogation go so much smoother and decrease the chance that he would be arrested.

"Oh, gosh, I don't know." He was silent a moment before blurting out, "Wait—I did stop to check my map after I'd hung up with Gloria. I remember because the rain had just started to pour down. I do recall stopping in front of the fountain when I was putting my map away."

Lana's heart sunk. She had been a few streets away from the fountain when it began to rain, meaning he could have already reached the Trevi by then. Which meant he could have been at the scene of the crime.

Randy gasped. "What if Rachel climbed up onto the fountain to try to get a better view of where I was going? What if she slid off one of the rocks and fell into the water?"

Lana held the phone away from her ear and stared at it in disbelief, before answering her friend. "Are you blaming yourself for Rachel's death? Snap out of it—you had nothing to do with it! Even if that's how she died, it wouldn't make it your fault. Hopefully, the police will find someone who saw what happened to her. They're also going to look at the surveillance videos taken in the vicinity. It's too bad it was raining so hard right then. Otherwise there would have been more people out on the streets."

"Lana, if the cops find out about Rachel and me fighting in the hotel lobby, and that she followed me to the station, then they might suspect I had something to do with her death. Dang it—I'm getting another call. I better answer it, especially if it's the police."

"Take care of yourself, Randy. I'm certain you'll be back with Gloria before breakfast."

"I hope you are right. Thanks for looking after my friends."

Lana hung up, wondering why she'd just lied to her friend. The chances that Randy would be back with his fiancée by morning were slim to none.

16

Legal Advice

"Hey, Dotty. Did I catch you at a bad time?" Lana asked.

"Course not. I always have time to chat with you. How is the trip going so far?"

"It's not as relaxing as we had hoped. Randy's ex-girlfriend Rachel showed up at our hotel and made a big scene last night."

Dotty gasped. "Do you mean the stalker?"

"How did you know about that? His friends told me about Rachel and what she did to him, but Randy's never mentioned it."

"He wanted me to know about her behavior and the restraining order before I hired him. He was worried she might show up at the office and start asking questions about his schedule. She called a few times and tried to wheedle information out of us, but once I made clear that I am on a first-name basis with Seattle's chief of police, she left us alone. I figured Randy's troubles with Rachel weren't anybody's business but his, so I promised not to say anything."

Lana felt horrible. Here she'd thought she and Randy were good friends. "I had no idea—he's never said a word about Rachel or having a stalker. He's such a friendly and upbeat guy. I guess that can be misinterpreted, at least by the wrong kind of woman."

"I didn't press him for details, but I know Gloria is terrified of Rachel. Which makes her showing up in Rome a major concern for everyone."

"Not anymore. The police found Rachel's body in the Trevi Fountain this morning."

"Oh, no! Drowning seems like a horrible way to die," Dotty cried.

"Frankly, every way seems pretty horrifying, when you think about it for too long. The rub is, I was there when the police pulled her out of the water, so they know why she was in Rome. They just finished interviewing me and Randy's friends and said they are going to pull Randy off the train and bring him back to Rome so they can question him further."

"But why question him? Randy didn't do anything wrong. Rachel is the psychopath."

"That fight in our hotel's lobby was pretty nasty and very public. At one point, he pushed Rachel away, and she cut her head open when she fell. Anyone who witnessed it would probably think Randy was the crazy one."

"What? I can't believe he pushed her like that. He doesn't seem the type. Though Rachel was a thorn in his side for so long, he must have snapped."

"I hope the police don't come to the same conclusion," Lana said glumly.

"Poor Randy. He should be worrying about his wedding, not answering police questions." Dotty was silent a moment before exclaiming, "I'll have to tell his parents what's going on. They are going to be so worried! And Gloria—how is she holding up?"

"I'm not sure; I wanted to call you first. I don't think she knows that the police are going to question Randy. As far as I know, he's not under arrest. But could you recommend an Italian lawyer, in case he needs legal help?"

"I'll ask my lawyers to recommend one," Dotty said before clicking her tongue. "Gloria is going to be a mess when she finds out. I'll give her a call, too, when we're done."

"That would be great if you did. Do you think it's better to continue the tour of Rome? Or should I cancel it?" Lana asked, knowing what her boss's answer would be.

"The tour must go on," Dotty said as Lana mouthed the words along with her.

"If any of his friends want to leave, then I'll help them change their tickets. But we have to assume Randy will be back at the vineyard in time for his wedding. As soon as the police talk to him, they'll come to their senses and release him," Dotty continued. "I cannot believe they would make him miss his wedding, unless they find definitive proof that he did it. Which I doubt they'll find—that boy catches spiders and takes them outside whenever he comes by, just so I don't squish them. He just doesn't have a killer's instinct."

"He was pretty angry about Rachel showing up, but you're right about him—Randy's not the murdering type. Yet, the police don't seem to think it was an accident. I hope they find a witness or surveillance videos that shed more light onto what happened to Rachel or who might have harmed her," Lana said.

She then drew in a deep breath and let her eyes close as she focused on her next, and possibly most painful, task. "Before I talk to Randy's friends, I have to call Alex and let him know that his brother is being questioned by the police."

"I hope it doesn't upset him too much."

"Oh, I'm quite certain it will. Alex takes his role as big brother quite seriously."

17

Brotherly Love

"I'm coming to Rome."

"Alex, you will lose your job if you walk out on your clients," Lana said, trying to reason with her boyfriend despite knowing that it was a waste of breath. He had that determined tone in his voice, the one that meant arguing with him was futile—his mind was made up.

"I don't care! I should have bowed out of this week's conference as soon as Randy told me about his wedding plans. And now this!" Alex raged.

Lana's heart went out to him, wishing she could somehow reassure him that it would all work out, so he didn't leave the conference early and get fired. "Sweetie, there's not much you can do for him right now. The police want to talk to him, they aren't arresting him. I know you two are close but—"

"Randy is my baby brother! I won't be able to concentrate on my work knowing he is in trouble. I'm coming to Rome. Period."

"We don't even know if Rachel was murdered yet. It might have been a crazy accident, especially if she climbed up onto the fountain."

"If the police do think Rachel was murdered, they won't look any further than Randy," Alex insisted. "I'm sure that's why they are taking him into custody. Foreigner kills foreigner is the best outcome for the Italian police. And once they find out about the restraining order and their fight in the lobby, they'll have even more reason to suspect Randy. They might not even consider the possibility that it was an accident."

"The lead investigator said they were collecting surveillance videos from shops in the vicinity. I have to believe that the police will be able to find out more about the last minutes of Rachel's life once they've reviewed them all. Hopefully one of the cameras caught her killer on tape—if she was indeed murdered."

"Randy is getting married in six days to the love of his life, and I am not going to sit around twiddling my thumbs, hoping the police release him in time. Rachel destroyed his life, and I'll be damned if she ruins his wedding, as well."

Lana hesitated a moment, letting him calm down before she asked a question she couldn't suppress any longer. "Alex, why didn't you ever tell me about Rachel?"

"Because Randy forbade us from talking about her. She's caused him so much pain, he couldn't bear to hear her name. All he wanted to do was forget about that chapter in his life."

"Okay, I get that. But we are in a committed relationship and do live together..."

"And you work with Randy. If I'd told you, you might have treated him differently or accidentally mentioned it. I'm not saying that you're a blabbermouth, but it's only human nature to want to know more. And you are more curious than most."

"I understand," Lana said, suppressing a grin. She did have trouble letting things go once they piqued her curiosity. And Alex was right; she would have had a difficult time not asking Randy about it. "I hope you aren't keeping any more secrets from me."

"Oh, hon, it was never my intention to keep anything from you. Rachel is Randy's business—not mine. Trust me, you know all of my secrets. I wouldn't have it any other way."

Lana felt a rush of warmth as she took in the sincerity in his voice. Alex was an incredible guy, and she was lucky to have found him. "Darling, when do you think you'll be arriving in Rome? I can meet you at the train station or airport."

"I love you, Lana Hansen," Alex said, his voice breaking with emotion. "I'm going to find my boss and tell him there's a family emergency and that I need to leave right away. With a little luck, he'll be compassionate and I won't lose my job. Either way, I'll do my best to get a train or flight from Lisbon and should be in Rome by tomorrow night. I'll let you know as soon as I have a ticket booked."

"Be safe. I love you." Lana held the phone to her chest, even after Alex hung up, grateful he was on his way to Rome.

18

Video Surveillance

December 19—Day Two of the Wanderlust Tour in Rome, Italy

"They've arrested Randy!" Gloria cried.

Lana pulled the phone back, her ear ringing from her friend's shrill cry, as she sat up straight in her bed. Gloria's call had woken her up from a deep slumber. By the time she'd gotten off the phone with Alex last night, it was one in the morning. Too exhausted to deal with anything else, she had called it a night, figuring everyone needed a good night's sleep before they decided what to do next. "Why? He didn't hurt Rachel."

"The police think he did. Several shops in the vicinity have security cameras, and the police viewed their surveillance tapes. They said they were tracing Rachel's movements and saw that she seemed to be following a man in a Straight Up Climbs jacket."

"Randy," Lana mumbled as she rubbed the sleep out of her eyes.

"Yes. Apparently the jacket made it easy for the police to find Randy in the video footage. They said they spotted Rachel following him towards the Trevi, but lost sight of both of them a block before they would have reached the fountain. They did find footage of Rachel ducking under a hotel's awning when it began to rain. It was one of the boutique hotels around the corner from the Piazza di Trevi."

"That's the little square in front of the fountain, right?"

"It is. The police claim a man wearing a Straight Up jacket grabbed Rachel's arm and pulled her in the direction of the Trevi. But the camera was hanging off a café to the left of the hotel, and the rain made it impossible for them to get a good look at the person's face."

"That doesn't sound good."

Gloria continued recounting her conversation with the police, as if she was in autopilot mode. "They don't have any video footage of the fountain itself, nor did they see anyone else interacting with Rachel. According to the cops, after Randy had disappeared from their view for about five minutes, they spotted him leaving the area, but not Rachel. That gap would have given him enough time to have killed her, the police think."

"That doesn't make any sense. Why didn't they check the rest of the cameras across from the Trevi? There are several cafés and hotels on that little square."

"That's what I said! The police claim most of the shops on the Piazza di Trevi don't have video surveillance. The only hotel that had a clear shot of the fountain is having trouble with its surveillance equipment. The bottom line is the police don't know exactly who attacked Rachel or how she ended up in the water. And they aren't going to let Randy go until they figure it out."

That poor woman, Lana thought. Gloria should be stressing about her wedding day, not about her husband getting arrested for murder.

"Wait a second—I was following them, too. Right before I reached the Trevi, it began to pour down rain. It was like someone turned on the shower, it was coming down so hard. That would have definitely affected the camera's visibility and must have made it more difficult for the police to track their movements. Randy did tell me that he stopped and checked his map when he reached the Trevi. Maybe that's why he supposedly disappeared from their view. Are they one hundred percent certain that the person they saw pulling Rachel away is Randy?"

"I don't think they are, but they won't admit it. When I pushed them about how they identified Randy in the video, they said through his Straight Up Climbs jacket. They don't have any close-ups of his face—just that blasted windbreaker. I told them that we are all wearing those jackets during this trip, but the police didn't seem to care. They know about the fight in the hotel lobby and Randy's restraining order. It sounds like they've already decided he did it and aren't going to bother to look for another suspect!" Gloria screamed and wept at the same time. "But those jackets are so loose-fitting, it could have been any one of them!"

Lana gulped as she realized what Gloria was saying. "So if Randy didn't do this—"

"One of his friends did," Gloria finished her thought. "It's horrible to think so, but I don't see any other explanation. It's not like one of our jackets was stolen. And the general public can't buy the version we were wearing—those are only available for guides. Heather had to beg the owner to let her order two for you and Craig."

"Gloria, I think I saw Heather and Jake following Randy, as well."

"You have to tell the police!"

"The cops already interviewed us, and they both denied seeing Rachel after that fight in the lobby."

"Why would they lie—unless it was one of them?"

Lana chewed on her lip as she considered Gloria's words. "I don't know. But they are Randy's best friends. Let me talk to them first, before I throw them to the wolves. There might be an easy explanation. For all we know, those two are romantically involved and were meeting up on the sly. What does Randy have to say about all of this?"

"The police won't let me talk to him directly, but they did tell me that he maintains that he did not see Rachel at any point during his walk."

"Why don't the police believe him? How can they keep him in custody if they have no proof that Randy knew Rachel was following him?"

Gloria was silent a moment before whispering, "Because of your voicemails, Lana. They convinced the police that Randy knew Rachel was following him. They think he waited for her in one of the small alleyways, attacked her when she ducked under that hotel awning, and then drowned her in the Trevi. Can you believe it?"

A wave of shame rolled over Lana, temporarily numbing her body and mind. *This is all my fault*, she thought. *If I hadn't identified Rachel, the police wouldn't have known why she was in Rome, and Randy would be helping Gloria hang up streamers for his wedding day instead of being locked up in a Roman jail cell.*

"No, I cannot. Randy wouldn't hurt a fly. Although..." Lana's voice trailed off as she recalled his violent confrontation with Rachel in the lobby.

Gloria cut in, as if she could read Lana's mind. "He told me about the incident at the hotel and how everyone in the lobby saw it happen. I couldn't believe it either, at first. Randy is not a violent person and he feels horrible for hurting her. But that woman turned our lives into a nightmare. The police think her showing up at his hotel could have pushed him over the edge. But I know he wouldn't have killed her, no matter how mad or upset he was! I don't understand why Rachel was following him, but he swears he didn't see or speak to her on the way to the station. For most of the walk, he was on the phone with me! I would have heard her voice if she'd tried to speak to him."

Lana paused a moment, feeling as if everything was spiraling out of control. "When Randy left the hotel, I noticed Rachel was following him, so I chased after him to warn him. He wasn't answering his phone because he was talking with you. But I kept losing sight of him, which is why I left those messages. If I had known my voicemails would help land him in prison, I never would have left them. You know that, don't you?"

"Of course I do. You were trying to help him, and we both appreciate it. No one could have known it would have come to this. Unfortunately, Randy was so mad that he erased your messages off his phone, which made the police even more suspicious. They reckon if he hit Rachel at the hotel, then it's entirely possible he did it again. It's as if they have already decided he murdered her and are viewing all of his actions in the most negative light possible. The police are never going to look for another suspect because they are certain they have her killer in custody. You have to help me prove Randy's innocence, Lana!"

Alex was right, Lana thought. The police were going to close this case without looking any further. "I'm certain Randy didn't do this, but do you honestly think one of his friends did? The police did say their suspect was wearing a Straight Up Climbs jacket."

Gloria sighed. "Honestly, I can't see any of them wanting to hurt her, either. It's hard to know for certain, but I suspect that we are the only ones in Rome with those jackets right now."

Lana blew out through her nose, disgusted by what she had to ask. "I'm going to need your help, Gloria. I don't know Randy's friends as well as you do. What can you tell me about them and their possible motives for wanting to hurt Rachel?"

When Gloria remained silent, Lana added, "What about Craig? He and Randy met at college, right?"

"Yes, they lived in the same dormitory for their first two years of college and hung out quite a bit. Randy said that they aren't as close as they used to be because Craig isn't interested in the outdoors anymore, and that's where Randy prefers to be when he's got time off. When Craig does show up at our parties, he usually keeps to himself. I know Randy only invited him to the wedding because he didn't want to hurt Craig's feelings, but we were both surprised when he said he was coming. But I can't imagine Craig harming Rachel. If anything, I would say Craig was in love with her. No, love is too strong—I'd say he's infatuated with her."

"What! Are you sure? He is one of Randy's oldest friends. You'd think he would have stayed away from her."

"She was a forbidden subject, but Craig let it slip a few times that he thought Randy treated Rachel badly. It was the way he said it that made me think he was interested in her, too. I don't know if they ever dated, but he does have a soft spot for her. But then again, most men do. I mean, did."

"What about Heather? She adores Randy and hated Rachel," Lana said.

"Heather did hate Rachel, but mostly because she wouldn't leave Randy alone after he broke up with her. I know Craig thinks Heather is in love with Randy, but I can't really recall her ever making a move on him. It's more like she considers Randy her big brother."

"It's odd—yesterday I got the feeling that Heather doesn't like you, but I can't remember her ever being rude to you before."

"No woman is ever good enough for your brother, are they?" Gloria sighed.

"Before we announced our engagement, Heather was nice to me, though never super friendly. Since Randy told her the news, she's been downright hostile and takes every opportunity to badmouth me. He thinks she's mad because he had less time to go hiking with her, but her nasty remarks are only pushing Randy away."

"And Jake—what's his story?" Lana asked.

"I don't really know much about him. He and Randy always meet up at the climbing hall and have a drink in their bar afterwards. Jake's been to a few of our parties, but he was too busy hitting on the hottest female in the room to have time for me. He does seem quite sure of himself, if you know what I mean."

Lana thought of his slightly arrogant manner. "Yes, I think I do. Did you know that Jake and Rachel were dating?"

"What?" Gloria gasped. "No, I did not. And I guarantee you that Randy didn't either; otherwise he wouldn't have invited Jake to our wedding. He was terrified Rachel would find out about it."

"Yeah, Randy does seem to think one of his friends told Rachel when and where the wedding was taking place."

"They must have—we only told those we were inviting, and only after they confirmed that they were coming. We wanted as few people to know where it was happening, as possible."

Lana was silent for a moment. "You know I love you both, but aren't you two being a bit paranoid?"

"In the past year, we have had to move twice and change our telephone numbers more times than I can count, just so she'll leave us alone. That restraining order helped a little, but not much."

Lana felt like a fool for thinking her friends were overreacting. She had believed Randy when he said that they'd found a better rental and wanted to move the next week, or that he'd found a cheaper telephone plan again and had to change his number. She had never considered that there was a sinister reason behind the frequent changes.

"I'm sorry for doubting you. You are right—I had no idea of what you two were going through. And here I thought I knew Randy well."

"It's not your fault; he didn't want to think about Rachel or be reminded of her in any way. Besides, he would have hated it if you felt sorry for him. It was easier for him to not tell anyone about it."

When Lana fell silent, contemplating his friends' motives, Gloria added, "Is there anyone else you have questions about? I need to talk to my parents about all of this."

"What about Katherine? How is it that she and Randy managed to stay friends?"

"After Randy dumped Rachel, Katherine switched the schedule around so that they wouldn't have to work together. I know Randy was quite grateful to her for that," Gloria explained.

"She doesn't seem too dismayed by her sister's death."

"I'm not surprised that Katherine's not upset. She'd been living in Rachel's shadow for so long. Katherine always told us that Rachel was the older, prettier sister whom their parents adored. I thought she was exaggerating or jealous, until their mother dropped by to take Rachel to lunch. When she found out that Rachel wasn't in the office, their mother didn't even ask Katherine if she would join her. Instead, she left without saying hello. It was pretty painful for everyone. When Rachel got back and heard what happened, she laughed in Katherine's face."

"Ouch. Talk about rubbing salt in the wound."

"Rachel was quite cruel to Katherine. She knew she was the family favorite and never let Katherine forget it. From what Randy said, she liked to steal away Katherine's boyfriends, too, which is why she didn't want Rachel to meet Bruce. Oh! I wonder what this will do to her—being the only daughter. I wonder how her parents are going to react."

"That is an excellent question. I'll keep an eye on Katherine. Grief can do strange things to a person. What do you know about Bruce?"

"Not much, to be honest. I know he and Katherine met when he worked as a guide one summer during college. But he's working as a computer programmer now and prefers kayaking to mountain climbing."

"A man after my own heart."

"Yes, well, he seems like a good guy. And he and Katherine are great together."

Lana was silent a moment as she contemplated all that Gloria had shared. Unfortunately, she didn't feel as if she'd learned anything new that could help her point to Rachel's true killer. "From what you've told me, it doesn't sound like anyone wanted Rachel dead."

"Maybe someone tried to rob or assault Rachel and it turned deadly. I don't understand how they got ahold of our jackets, but I do know Randy didn't do this," Gloria wailed. "Yet until we can find a reason for the police to doubt his involvement, they won't look for another suspect."

"I'll keep my ears open today, and Alex will be here tonight. I promise we'll do everything we can to set Randy free."

19

Investigating Friends

As soon as Lana hung up the phone, she fired up her trusty laptop. It was time to find out more about Randy's good friends. The thought made her slightly nauseated—what kind of friend would do this to him? Just like Gloria, Lana was certain that Randy would not have killed Rachel, as much as he may have wanted to. Heck, if he'd caused her to fall into the water, he was the kind of guy who would have stopped to help her back out again.

But if one of his friends had harmed Rachel, they must know that their continued silence would cause Randy not only to miss his wedding day, but also to spend several years in an Italian prison.

After she opened an internet browser, Lana's fingers hovered over the keyboard as she tried to decide who to investigate first. Before she looked into a specific person, she wanted to find out more about Randy's accident and its official cause. It seemed to be a recurring theme on this tour and the reason why Randy was terrified of Rachel.

She soon found a short article about his ladder's collapse that confirmed the details provided by Randy's friends. The safety catch broke while Randy was climbing over a crevasse on Disappointment Cleaver, causing the ladder to fold in the middle. The unexpected movement threw him off balance, and his leg got caught in between the rungs. When the ladder slammed against the ice wall, it fractured his ankle, calf, and knee.

Lana sat back, stunned that her friend had gone through this experience yet never really opened up about it with her. She'd known that he had gone through intensive physical therapy and still walked with a slight limp, but he'd always been vague about the details of his accident.

She finished reading the last few paragraphs, learning that the official cause of Randy's fall was equipment failure. Both Heather and Rachel were suspended until an insurance investigation could determine whether either was to blame. Lana was unable to find a follow-up article.

Lana tapped her chin, thinking back to the conversation she'd had with Randy's friends about his fall. Why hadn't anyone mentioned that Heather was also temporarily suspended? His friends had been quite keen to tell her all about Randy's suspicions concerning Rachel's possible involvement. Were they simply afraid of humiliating Heather by telling Lana about it?

That must be it, she thought, deciding that she would have to ask the younger woman about her suspension. As much as she didn't want to embarrass her, Randy's freedom was far more important than staying on Heather's good side.

The equipment specialist was Lana's first target. She soon discovered the bubbly blonde had worked for Straight Up Climbs for eleven years, which meant she and Randy had started their jobs around the same time. Was that coincidence, or had Heather taken the job in order to be closer to Randy?

It was painfully clear that Heather longed to be a part of Randy's life, though Lana still wasn't certain that the young woman wanted to be his romantic partner. They had known each other for so long that they had literally grown up together. Lana could imagine that Heather didn't want to lose that closeness once he married.

When she searched further, Lana stumbled upon a plethora of articles in which Heather was mentioned. Apparently she was also an environmental activist and had been arrested twice during protests held in downtown Seattle. Lana was shocked to read about the tiny blonde's fierce resistance to the police—and to see a photo of Heather biting an officer as he tried to handcuff her. *She is even more spirited and impassioned than I realized*, Lana thought.

Next up was Craig. He was extremely active on social media and shared moments from his personal life on a daily basis. To celebrate his friend's upcoming marriage, Craig had recently posted forty photos of him and Randy, taken during their university days. Lana chuckled at their clothes and goofy grins as she quickly scanned the images. Craig was the most changed, considering his full mane of dark hair in the photos. Randy's hair was shaggy and long, similar to how he wore it now. Several photos featured women that Lana assumed were the two men's then-girlfriends, considering the close embraces and kissing faces.

Although most of Craig's posts received many thumbs up, Randy hadn't liked or commented on any of them. However, Lana knew that Randy preferred spending his free time outdoors rather than on social media.

When Lana was done reviewing Craig's photos, something niggled at her brain, telling her to take another look. During this second pass, she noticed what was bothering her. Three of the women she'd noticed cuddling with Craig were also photographed kissing Randy. When she checked the dates in each case, Craig was with the women in earlier shots, only to be replaced by Randy several weeks later. *What strange photos to share*, Lana thought; it was as if Craig was reminding everyone that Randy ended up dating his old girlfriends.

Lana wasn't certain she liked the Randy that Craig shared with his Facebook friends. Was Randy the instigator of the breakups? Or was it pure coincidence? During their first breakfast together, Craig did tell them that he'd bumped into an old flame at the airport, one who dumped him to date Randy. It appeared to be a pattern.

Had Craig also been involved with Rachel when Randy met her? From what she could recall, Randy had said they'd met at Straight Up Climbs. But maybe Lana was remembering it wrong and they'd met via Craig instead. She would have to ask Craig about it.

When Lana ticked "Rachel Merriweather" into the Facebook search engine, a light shiver ran up her back. It almost felt as if she was summoning the dead. If Rachel and Craig had been involved, Lana expected to find some sort of photographic evidence on social media. Rachel seemed the type to post about herself on an hourly basis.

Unfortunately, she was right. It appeared that Rachel had taken a selfie with pretty much everyone she met and posted pics several times a day. It was eerie to see her laughing and smiling for the camera.

Jake had said that they'd met a month ago, and from the looks of Rachel's social media, he wasn't lying. Most of the more recent snaps were of her and Jake, cuddling and kissing while partying in a host of expensive-looking bars and restaurants. Lana was about to click away when a blurry image taken in a Seattle nightclub a few weeks earlier made her hand freeze. This one wasn't of Jake, but of Craig and Rachel in a passionate embrace. "Look who I ran into!" was the caption.

"What the heck?" Lana mumbled. Maybe Craig and Rachel were romantically involved, as well. It seemed like every man alive was drawn to her. Well, except for Randy.

Lana made a note to ask Craig about his relationship with Rachel, knowing she would need to speak with him in private about it. If he had been dating Rachel, she could imagine he would rather that Jake not find out.

She scrolled through the photos Rachel had posted in the past six months, but couldn't find any more images of either man, so she turned her attention back to Craig, digging further into his life. He worked as an architect at a small firm in Ballard, a neighborhood in Seattle close to Lana's home in Fremont. Other than posting about parties he'd attended and restaurants he'd eaten at, Craig didn't share much about his current interests—assuming he had any.

Next up was Katherine, Randy's friend and former coworker. From what Lana could find online, Katherine was five years younger than Rachel and had been working for Straight Up Climbs for six years. Beyond that, she was a mystery. Her social media was limited to sporadic photos of her and Bruce, but nothing more. Lana was slightly surprised that there were no photos of her sister or parents, but from what the others said, they didn't get along that well.

Her boyfriend, Bruce, was as much of an enigma. Though Katherine tagged him in several shots, his Facebook page didn't even have a profile photo, and he wasn't active on any other social media. Lana was shocked, yet pleased.

She'd always thought a robust social media presence was a requirement for Millennials and that Randy was the exception. It was good to see that not everyone under thirty was obsessed with that virtual world.

Jake was her last target and the person she knew the least about. They'd met at one of Randy's parties, but he had been too busy chatting up the single ladies to really notice her. Given his muscular build and rugged good looks, Lana wouldn't be surprised if his advances were successful most of the time.

When she ticked his name into her internet browser, a long list of links appeared. She opened his Instagram account and found several photos of him and Randy that he'd recently taken in a local climbing hall. They really did love to climb together, and often, it seemed. *Funny how Randy didn't have time to get together with Heather, but did make time for Jake*, Lana mused. Perhaps he was unconsciously distancing himself from his female friends.

She then went back to the list of links. The earliest articles were about his successes in track and field at the University of Oregon and the many medals he'd earned. Things seemed to have gone well for him until he hit his senior year. Jake was arrested for assaulting a female student during a back-to-school celebration. Although the details about his crime weren't mentioned in the article, he was promptly booted out of the university. From what Lana could tell, he didn't attend another one.

The next mention of Jake was three years later and in reference to another altercation—this time while working in a Chicago nightclub as a security guard. He got grabby with a female patron, and after she slapped him with her purse, he punched her in the jaw and broke it in two.

Lana's eyes widened in disbelief. What kind of person was this? She tried to reconcile the casual, easygoing guy Randy had introduced her to with this monster she was reading about. Granted, the last article was dated six years ago. Maybe the incident was all a horrible misunderstanding, she thought, though two references to assault made that unlikely. Unfortunately, she couldn't find any more details about his arrests or punishment.

Lana sat back against her bed's headboard, frustrated. There wasn't much to find out about Randy's friends because they were all who they said they were. Only Jake's alleged assaults were something she needed help investigating.

Considering she had no other leads at the moment, Lana checked her world clock. It wasn't too late in Seattle to call her ex-boss and good friend, Jeremy. She figured it was a long shot, but right now she had no idea who would have wanted Rachel dead—other than Randy.

Jeremy had been Lana's editor when they worked at the *Seattle Chronicle*, one of the city's most important daily newspapers. When Lana was wrongly fired for having committed libel, Jeremy was also let go. After she'd been cleared of any wrongdoing, the newspaper had offered Jeremy his old job back, just as they did Lana. Both turned the newspaper down, Lana because she was happy being a guide and writing her travel blog, and Jeremy because he was happy working at a smaller, regional newspaper. The hours were better now that he had three daughters to raise.

She dialed his number, confident he would be able to find out more about Jake's criminal past.

"Hey Jeremy, how are you doing?" Lana asked in the most cheerful voice possible when he answered. They were good friends, but she still hated getting him involved in her off-the-cuff investigations, knowing how little free time he had for his family. However, she also knew from previous experiences how much he enjoyed burrowing down to the truth and helping her catch a killer.

"Great," he said. "In fact, I haven't felt this good in years. The kids are staying with my parents for the week. Kitty and I have had to work so much overtime these past few days, we didn't know how we were going to juggle our schedules. Luckily, Mom offered to take the kids off our hands. The grandparents love pampering the girls, who love having so much attention, and we can get our work done without having to burn the candle at both ends. It's a win-win for all of us, frankly. We'll have to arrange more of these sleepovers in the future."

"I am so glad to hear that," Lana replied. She knew that Jeremy's wife, Kitty, had recently started a new job at a local microbrewery and they were all still adjusting to her working full time instead of being a stay-at-home mom. "Say, listen, since you have so much free time on your hands, could I ask a favor?"

Jeremy groaned. "I'm almost afraid to ask what it is."

Lana winced, feeling like a heel for ruining his good mood. "I wouldn't ask, but Randy is in police custody and—"

"Randy, as in the guy who's about to get married? What happened?"

"Yep, one and the same. His ex-girlfriend turned up in Rome yesterday, they had a nasty fight in public, and she was found dead in the Trevi Fountain late last night."

"That's heavy."

"I know. I'm sure it's all a misunderstanding, but the police arrested him last night, and we are afraid they won't look for other suspects now that they have Randy in custody."

"So you decided to take the lead?" Jeremy said in a teasing voice.

"Yes, well, Randy is Alex's baby brother. I'm doing a background check of the other guests to see if anyone else might have wanted Rachel dead. So far, I've come up with nothing sordid about any of them, with the possible exception of a guy named Jake Segers. It looks like he has been in trouble with the law in Oregon and Illinois, and I would love to know more about the incidents, charges, and punishment. Could you maybe ask one of your police reporters to check him out?"

"Anything for Randy, especially if it will help get him to the altar on time. I'll call my crime desk editor right away. She'll get her team on it."

Lana released the breath she didn't know that she'd been holding in. "Thanks so much, Jeremy. I really appreciate this, and I know Randy and his fiancée do, too."

"If you really want to thank me, get me two tickets to one of your fancy tours. Kitty and I haven't been on vacation in years, and those Wanderlust packages are way too expensive for my meager salary."

"It's a deal. After all you've done to help me out, I'll work something out with Dotty."

Lana could hear him smiling through the phone. "Will you give me a ring when you find out more?"

"Of course. Talk soon."

20

Checking In

"Hey gang, how are you holding up?" Lana asked Randy's friends, now gathered together in Katherine and Bruce's hotel room. Heather had called to let Lana know that they would wait for her there, before heading down to breakfast.

When Lana knocked on the door, she had expected to see everyone still reeling from the news of Rachel's death. Yet no one seemed overly distraught this morning. Bruce sat against one bed's headboard with Katherine in his arms. Jake was perched on the end of the other one. Heather and Craig sat in the two chairs placed next to a small table.

Could one of them really be the killer? Or was Rachel's death a terrible accident? The missing wallet and figure in a Straight Up Climbs jacket made the latter unlikely.

After investigating all of their backgrounds, Lana felt a little funny in their presence, even though she'd found out nothing sordid about the most of them. Jake was the one exception, and she could feel the hair on the back of her neck standing on end as she looked sideways towards him. Yet until Jeremy found out more about his background, she could not treat him differently. For all she knew, he had been taken into custody but released without being charged. Neither of the newspaper articles provided many details about the incidents. Craig appeared to be uncomfortable in Jake's presence as well, Lana noted, as he twisted into a strange sitting position so that the mountaineering guide was out of his vision.

"I never liked Rachel, so don't expect me to be sorry that she's gone," Heather growled.

"We're okay, Lana, but I would love to be distracted from all of this," Katherine said. "Did you have anything planned for today?"

"How can you think about sightseeing? What about Randy—shouldn't we be trying to help him?" Heather pressed.

"What do you mean? The police are questioning him; they didn't arrest him," Bruce said.

"Well, actually, there has been a new development," Lana replied. "Gloria just called to tell me the police did arrest Randy."

"What? Why!" Heather cried.

"Because of the video footage they'd found. In it, they can see Rachel being pulled towards the Trevi by a man they believe is Randy." Lana couldn't bear to tell them that her voicemail messages helped to land him in jail. The fact that the suspected killer was wearing a Straight Up jacket was also a point Lana felt she'd better keep to herself for the time being. If one of them was responsible for Rachel's death, that clue might alert them to be on their guard. And Randy was supposed to be getting married in five days—there was no time to lose.

"The owner of Wanderlust Tours is going to find him a lawyer," Lana added. "We simply don't believe he killed Rachel, intentionally or accidentally. If he had pushed her in the water, he would have helped her out—no matter how mad he was."

Heather nodded emphatically as she rubbed at her red-rimmed eyes. "That's the kind of guy Randy is."

Craig snorted. "You could have fooled me. He shoved Rachel pretty hard back at the hotel."

"Because she pushed and pushed and pushed, until he lost it. Rachel was a sick person," Katherine stated.

"The police were quite vague about what exactly they saw on that video, and it doesn't sound like they have footage taken at the Trevi," Lana continued. "We're keeping our fingers crossed that his lawyer can sort this out, preferably before his wedding day."

"It must have been an accident," Bruce insisted. "Who would have wanted Rachel dead?"

A wave of sadness washed over Jake's face. Lana suspected he was more in love with Rachel than he'd originally let on.

Katherine untangled herself from her boyfriend's embrace and plopped down next to Jake on the other bed. "We didn't always get along, but she was my sister. I wouldn't have murdered her, no matter how much I may have wanted to."

The evil glare she shot back at her boyfriend confused Lana. *What in the world did Bruce do to deserve that?* she wondered. And what was with the unsolicited plea of innocence? No one was suggesting she may have harmed her sister.

"I didn't hurt Rachel, if that's what your look is implying," Bruce replied in an annoyed tone when he noticed the rest were watching him intently. "What about Jake? Maybe he got jealous of Rachel's obsession with Randy."

"Why would I have harmed her? You were there when we talked to the cops—we were dating. I had no reason to be jealous of anyone; I'd already landed the babe. Randy was the fool for letting her go," Jake said firmly.

Lana was astounded by their reactions. Why did they all feel the need to assure the others that they hadn't harmed Rachel?

"Randy is the only one of us who would have wanted to hurt her," Jake continued. "I know none of us want to consider it, but if Rachel confronted him, he may have hit her—in a fit of anger, of course. He had already done it once. And he's under a lot of pressure right now, with the wedding and all."

Lana looked at Jake through narrowed eyes. He was one to talk about hitting women.

"I know Randy didn't do this, no matter what evidence the police come up with," Heather said resolutely. "But I know none of us did, either. Rachel was a tease who loved to be in control. She probably flirted with a tourist, it got out of hand, and the stranger pushed her into the water. I wouldn't be surprised if we never find out who killed her."

Lana nodded along, knowing that what Heather said was a lie. Whoever pulled Rachel towards the Trevi was wearing one of their jackets.

She began tapping her toe, unable to hold in her curiosity any longer. However, when she opened her mouth to ask Heather whether she had been following Rachel or Randy that night, the younger woman turned on Jake.

"You must not know Randy as well as you think you do. If you did, you would know that he couldn't harm a soul. Even after all those horrid things that Rachel did to him, he still didn't want her dead—just out of his life."

"Okay, everybody. We all care about Randy, otherwise we wouldn't be here." Lana raised her voice as she glared at Jake and Heather. "Now that he's been arrested, we need to decide what we want to do—stay in Rome or go home?"

"Stay, of course. The police will soon see that Randy didn't do this and he'll be released in time for his wedding." Heather was adamant.

Lana looked to the rest, and they all nodded in agreement.

"Well, what are we waiting for? There's no point moping around here. We only have two days to explore Rome before we leave for Florence," Katherine said.

Lana jumped up, energized by their positivity. "Let me check today's itinerary and see what time our first tour starts. I'll be right back."

As soon as Lana was outside, she texted Dotty, "Tour going ahead as planned."

Seconds later, her boss responded with a smiley emoji and a thumbs up. "Well done—keep me informed!"

"Will do," Lana replied, then set off for her room.

94

21

Heavenly Artwork

The Vatican Museums were far larger and grander than Lana had imagined. She had not realized before coming that they housed the world's largest collection of art, much of which had been purchased or commissioned by the popes who had once lived within this city-state's walls.

The artwork had been divided into twenty-six museums, spread across fourteen hundred rooms, chapels, galleries, and gardens. The lavishly decorated spaces were filled with exquisite art, archeology, and ethnography. Each room was in itself a work of art, and no surface seemed to have been left untouched. The ceilings and walls were richly painted, chandeliers made of glass and precious metals hung everywhere, and swaths of intricately designed fabrics covered the windows and floors. Most rooms were dedicated to a different style of furnishing and artwork—from classical sculptures up to contemporary paintings by living artists. Walking from one space to the next was a sensory experience that bordered on overload. All of the rooms left her heart singing, though the presence of so much history and beauty was making her head spin.

Standing under the heavenly ceiling of the Sistine Chapel was certainly a highlight of her trip. Lana could have stared for hours at Michelangelo's masterpiece, a visual depiction of several scenes from the Bible's Old Testament. Lana's favorite was the *Creation of Adam*, a scene gracing the center of the ceiling, in which God reached out to touch Adam's finger.

Unfortunately, she was not the only one. Guards dotted around the hall constantly reminded visitors not to sit or take pictures, but instead to view the paintings and then leave so others could enter. Still, the chapel was a highlight of the afternoon.

It was only too bad that the group didn't seem to be enjoying it as much as she was. Today, their dynamic was off, and the atmosphere felt wrought with tension. Was it their conversation in Katherine's room this morning that had set everyone on edge?

Jake was more quiet than she remembered him normally being, but then again, he was dealing with the loss of a girlfriend. Craig wasn't making things easier for him. Whenever Jake opened his mouth, Craig was ready with a mean gibe. His snarling remarks were making everyone uncomfortable.

Why was Craig being so rude? He barely knows Jake, Lana thought. They obviously knew each other via Randy, yet it didn't sound like Jake was a regular at Randy's parties, but more of a climbing buddy. And Craig had no interest in climbing, biking, or hiking. He was more at home in a museum or library, she reckoned. She doubted the two men had ever had a real conversation.

Heather was also far more somber than her usual bubbly self. Her brow was knitted fast, and she was constantly checking her telephone for new messages, as if she expected Randy to get in touch at any moment. The fact that he was currently in police custody seemed too much for her to deal with.

They exited the Vatican Museums via a winding staircase that reminded Lana of a snail's shell. She walked out of the building, feeling at peace with the world. Then the doors to the outside world opened, and the beeping traffic of downtown Rome brought her crashing back down to earth.

They circled along the high walls surrounding Vatican City to Saint Peter's Square and joined the long lines of visitors wishing to enter Saint Peter's Church. Swiss Guard members dressed in what looked like colorful pajamas stood at attention by metal detectors and x-ray machines that checked everyone. Lana could hardly believe that it was free to enter, but then again, it was the most important place of worship to millions of Catholics. Charging all of those pilgrims an entrance fee did seem unfair.

Last night's sudden downpour had kicked off a night of rain that was luckily now a soft drizzle. When the drops increased again in intensity, several of those in line popped open their umbrellas, forcing visitors to give each other more space. Lana wished her Straight Up jacket had a hood; she had left her umbrella on her hotel bed. She never forgot things like that; Randy's arrest was throwing her off balance in more ways than one.

While they slowly snaked their way across Saint Peter's Square, Katherine made a show of photographing the incredible colonnade of two hundred and eighty-four columns surrounding the space, and the massive statues of the apostles mounted on top of it.

"Did you know that Bernini designed the columns, fountains, and statues?" Katherine said, sighing in happiness as she turned slowly, taking in the magnificent architecture surrounding them. "This was the top destination on my list of places to visit."

"Great choice, Kat. It's really quite spectacular. Did you notice anything strange about that nativity scene—the one next to the obelisk?" Bruce asked as he pointed to the massive holiday décor set up next to an Egyptian obelisk and a Christmas tree standing in the center of the square.

Katherine would have to be blind not to see it, Lana thought; the nativity scene was one of the largest she'd ever seen. The buildings and figurines were life-sized, and the entire decoration was brightly lit with stars and a comet hanging above an empty manger.

"There's no baby Jesus in the crib yet," Bruce said without waiting for his girlfriend to guess. "The figurines are added to the display as they happen, so Jesus appears on Christmas Eve and the Wise Men don't show up until January 6."

"I didn't know that!" Katherine replied enthusiastically as she stepped closer to the railing and zoomed her camera in on the religious display.

With Bruce and Katherine distracted, Lana saw her chance to find out why Heather and Jake had been following Randy. Yet with Craig present, she would have to tread carefully. Luckily, he had pulled out a guidebook and seemed to be boning up on the church they were about to see. She hoped he would be too distracted to follow their exchange.

"How was dinner, Heather?"

"Delicious," she responded immediately but avoided Lana's gaze as she answered.

"I'm not normally a fan of pesto, but theirs was pretty good," Jake added.

Craig looked up from his book, a snide expression on his face. "Are you a food critic now, too? You excel at everything, don't you?"

Jake looked away and ignored his barb.

Lana shook her head. What was with Craig's annoying remarks? Ever since Rachel died, he had been at Jake's throat. Craig's comments were grating on her nerves; she could imagine Jake was getting sick of them, too. But Jake seemed to just take it and made no attempt to respond verbally or physically.

"I heard you mention food. Were you telling Lana about dinner? It was a wonderful restaurant, wasn't it?" Katherine asked as she and Bruce rejoined them.

"It was heavenly. Thanks for the recommendation, Lana," Bruce said.

"It's too bad you couldn't make it," Katherine added. Oddly enough, she seemed to look past her. Given her new burst of self-confidence, Lana had expected Katherine to have made eye contact.

"Yeah, well, it sounds like Lana was busy helping the police," Heather cut in.

Katherine's eyebrows furrowed at Heather's remark. "I meant, all—"

"Speaking of food, I'm starving. After we see this church, I would love to grab some lunch. Lana, do you have any recommendations for a good café in the neighborhood, or should we keep our eyes open while we're walking around?" Jake asked as he patted his belly.

"This church? As if it's an insignificant—" Craig exploded.

Lana talked over him. "We can walk around and see what looks good when we're done. There are a whole bunch of restaurants in this neighborhood so we shouldn't have trouble finding a place to eat," she said to Jake, before grabbing Craig's arm and pulling him to the back of their group.

"Hey, Craig, are you doing alright?" she whispered. They were stuck in line so couldn't sneak away to talk privately, but it was so noisy with tourists and traffic that it was easy enough to create a few seconds alone.

"Yeah, I'm fine," he said, though his eyes were boring a hole into Jake's back.

"You don't seem alright. What's your beef with Jake?"

Craig whipped around to face her, and his expression softened. "Is it that obvious?"

"Ah, yeah," Lana said sarcastically. "What happened between you two?"

"I've never been a fan of Jake, that's all."

"Really? You didn't seem to have a problem with him until he told the police that he and Rachel had been dating. Were you going out with her, too? Is that what this is all about?"

Craig blushed and averted his gaze.

"I'll take that as a yes. So when did you date Rachel?"

Craig leaned in close, Lana assumed to ensure the rest couldn't hear their conversation. "We were never a couple, but we did go out a few times soon after Randy broke up with her. But I haven't seen her in months."

Lana knew he wasn't telling the truth because she had seen Rachel's photos. She let his lie slide for now, asking instead, "Did Randy know that you two were seeing each other?"

"No," he hissed, "Randy would not have invited me to the wedding if he did. Heck, I doubt he would ever want to speak to me again if he found out."

"You had better tell me what happened. Did you two date long?"

"Not at all. After Randy broke up with her, she started calling and texting me, saying that she had always liked me and now she was free to ask me out. It was flattering. Rachel was a beautiful woman."

"And your friend's ex. Didn't that bother you?"

"It never bothered Randy," Craig snapped back. "Do you know how many girls I lost to him? He didn't do it intentionally, but Randy is the kind of guy that women want to be with. And after they broke up, Rachel asked me out! It was the first time someone who had once been interested in him turned out to show an interest in me. I was thrilled beyond belief, not bothered."

Lana narrowed her eyes and started to respond when Craig added, "It doesn't matter; she wasn't really interested in me. She was using me to keep tabs on Randy, and after I stopped sharing anything about him with her, she dumped me."

"Then why were you two snuggling at the Crocodile Café three weeks ago?"

Craig's face drained of color. "What?"

"Rachel posted a photo of you two on her Facebook page. You looked pretty close to me."

"Oh, no! I sure hope Randy doesn't see it. No, we were definitely not dating," Craig whispered back.

"Then what were you doing?"

"We bumped into each other at the Crocodile Café, and she offered to buy me a beer. I figured it was serendipitous, us running into each other like that. I should have known it was a setup. I now know from Jake's conversation with the police that she and he were already dating, which means Rachel wasn't interested in me at all, at least not romantically. She was just using me to get to Randy again."

Lana felt her stomach tighten. "What happened exactly?"

"After a bit of chitchatting and flirting, she asked if I was still in touch with Randy. It made me so mad that I blurted out that he and Gloria were getting married. I thought if she knew he was off the market that she'd stop obsessing about him. How wrong I was."

"What do you mean?"

"I figured she would be shocked by my news, but she already knew he was getting married on Christmas Eve and about our trip to Rome. She wanted to know the name of Gloria's village. I bet Jake told her about the wedding and she came running to me to find out where, figuring Randy would have confided in his old friend. After I let it slip that Randy hadn't told anyone where it was being held, she called it a night, and I never heard from her again—until she showed up here in Rome."

"Oh, Craig," Lana murmured. He looked so forlorn, Lana felt bad for him.

He smirked and shook his head. "You know what hurt the most? As Rachel left, she made a nasty comment about how I must not be such great friends with Randy anymore if I didn't know where his wedding was taking place. I was so angry with Randy because of that. I know we've grown apart, but I always thought he trusted me. Now I understand why he didn't confide in anyone. Rachel is so manipulative; if he had told me, she would have gotten it out of me."

Poor guy, Lana thought. It seemed that whenever Randy was involved, Craig came in second place. Yet Lana simply couldn't see him harming Rachel, at least not intentionally. Why would he—because she wasn't interested in him? Craig had no motive to harm her otherwise, and that seemed like a silly reason to kill someone.

Craig touched her arm, his eyes pleading with her to take him seriously. "Promise me you won't tell Randy! He would never forgive me for staying in contact with Rachel."

What would I gain by doing so? she thought, realizing quickly that nothing good would come from Craig telling Randy the truth about his relationship with Rachel.

"I promise," she said solemnly. Before she could cross him off her mental list of suspects, Lana had to know one more thing. "Craig, did you harm Rachel?"

He shook his head. "I know she could be cruel and manipulative, but she could also be the kindest, sweetest woman on the face of the earth when she wanted to be. I could never have hurt her."

"Do you think Randy could have?"

"No way! Randy is not a violent person. Him pushing Rachel away was uncharacteristic, to say the least, but I know he didn't mean to and can imagine he felt horrible for doing so."

Lana considered his words, before finally nodding in agreement.

"Are we done here?" Craig asked.

"What did you do after Randy and Rachel fought in the hotel lobby? Did you walk over to the café with the others?"

"No, I wanted to see the Basilica of Santa Maria in Trastevere before dinner, but the others weren't interested. So I left early and walked over to it before meeting up with them at the café."

Lana scanned his face, checking his sincerity.

"Here, let me show you the pictures I took." He pulled out his phone's camera and flipped through several photos of the colorful mosaics covering much of the medieval church's interior. She tapped on one photo, checking the date and time. Craig was telling the truth—while he was taking those pictures, she had been trailing after Rachel and Randy on the other side of town.

"And after you visited this church, you went straight to the café for dinner?"

"Yes."

"Was everyone already there by the time you arrived?"

"No, only Bruce and Katherine were there. They seemed a little perturbed that I interrupted their romantic dinner, but hey, you reserved one table for all of us."

"What do you mean—when did Heather and Jake show up?"

"Let's see, Jake showed up after we had been served our main course. I remember because they had to rush to make one for him, too. It was a set menu."

"And Heather?"

"She didn't arrive until we finished our dessert. Too bad for her, it was a scrumptious meal. She really missed out."

"Okay, thanks. Hey, one more thing, then I'll let you be."

Craig stiffened.

"Don't worry, it's an easy question to answer, I hope. Why did you share all those photos of you and Randy kissing the same women?"

Craig grimaced. "If you look closely, you'll notice Randy was doing the kissing, not me. They weren't my girlfriends, but women I was interested in. They all fell for Randy instead of me. I was more friend material, apparently."

Lana pursed her lips and nodded, embarrassed for him, yet relieved to know that Randy had not made a habit of stealing his friend's girlfriends.

Before she could ask anything else, Craig scurried forward in the line and stood close to Bruce, who was telling everyone about his favorite Italian foods.

As Lana watched the friends chatting casually, she found it almost impossible to believe that one of them could be Rachel's killer. Yet it must be one of them—their jackets pointed to someone in their group, not a random stranger.

She could definitely scratch Craig off her list of suspects. So where did that leave her investigation? Lana set her sights on Jake. She wanted to know why he'd betrayed Randy by telling Rachel about the location and date of his upcoming marriage.

22

Walking Among The Holy

By the time they wound their way through the snaking line and entered Saint Peter's Basilica, Lana was fuming. Had Jake really told Rachel about the wedding? He was supposed to be Randy's friend. Why on earth would he do so, knowing Randy was trying to keep its location a secret?

However, one look inside the church cleared her heart and mind of the anger and helplessness she was feeling, and replaced it with serenity and hope. Saint Peter's Basilica was truly the most impressive religious structure she had ever seen. The vaulted ceilings were stories high and held up by a rib cage of stone pillars decorated so lavishly that they seemed to blend into the floor and walls. Its roof was so much higher than a normal church's, and simply standing underneath it made Lana feel tiny and insignificant.

Rising like a tree from the building's center was the Papal Altar. Curving black pillars of wood held up a tent-like canopy, topped by a globe and the cross. It stood in front of a recessed circular staircase that led down to the cavernous crypts.

Soaring about the altar was a glorious dome made of windows and paintings. Streams of sunlight lit up the colorful portraits of popes, apostles, angels, and saints decorating it. Massive tombs dedicated to the popes matched the size of the chapel. The larger-than-life sculptural representations of these holy men were forever towering over the visitors and pilgrims gathered around their feet. Lana walked slowly past the masterfully carved sculptures of apostles and popes, taking in the fluidity of motion captured in stone and wood.

Visiting the church was a heavenly experience, yet Lana's brain was beginning to go into sensory overload. She completed her initial walk around the building, absorbing the enormity of the artwork—both in the literal and spiritual sense—before circling back to Michelangelo's *Pietà*. This majestic portrayal of Mary holding her dead son was the reason why Lana wanted to come here. There was something so tragic yet serene in Mary's expression as she tenderly comforted her only child.

The statue was placed quite close to the main entrance, meaning there was a constant stream of visitors trying to start their tour there. Lana joined the back of the crowd, patiently waiting to get closer to the marble masterpiece. When a large group entered and immediately pushed their way to the front, Lana stepped away, deciding to come back to the *Pietà* later. There was still plenty more to see.

When she turned around, her eyes passed over Jake, who was playing with his phone. She strode over to him. "Hey, how are you holding up?"

He looked at Lana with a perplexed expression on his face. "Fine, thanks."

"I can imagine it must be difficult to process your girlfriend's death."

His eyes widened in surprise before his lips pulled down. "Yeah, it's been tough. I mean, I thought we were going to have a romantic week in Rome together, and now, she's gone."

"Yeah, I bet." Considering Randy's wedding was taking place in days, not weeks, Lana decided to take the abrupt approach. "So Jake, if you knew the wedding was supposed to be a secret, why did you tell Rachel about it?"

Jake's head jolted back. "What are you talking about?" he whispered, but wouldn't meet her gaze. "I didn't tell her—who gave you that idea?"

He lied so sincerely, it was scary. He appeared to be truly offended.

"Craig told me about how Rachel tried pumping him for information about the wedding. It seems she already knew the date and country, just not the exact location."

Although Jake remained silent, his chiseled jaw tightened.

"Stop lying! We're in a church, for goodness' sake. You might be struck down if you keep it up."

His shoulders slumped. "I didn't know about her and Randy."

A security guard, one of many roaming the vast space, approached them from behind.

"No talking," the guard whispered and pointed to a prominent sign calling for silence.

Lana mouthed "Sorry" to the guard, then crooked her finger at Jake. She led them away from the *Pietà* and towards the bathrooms.

"Why did you tell Rachel about the wedding?" Lana hissed.

"How was I supposed to know she and Randy were ever an item? No one told me about them. Apparently it's a forbidden subject."

Lana glared at him, considering his words. Randy didn't know that Rachel was going to start working at Straight Up Climbs again, meaning he wouldn't have known that she and Jake could have met. And if Randy had never mentioned Rachel to her, then the chance that he had told Jake about his stalker was slim to none.

Was it coincidence that Rachel and Jake had recently started dating? Possibly, but this was Rachel—by all accounts an extremely manipulative young woman. If she knew that Jake and Randy were acquainted, then she might have asked him out in order to find out more about her old flame. After all, she had done the same thing to Craig.

"Did Rachel know that you and Randy were friends?"

"I don't know—she could have…" Jake's voice trailed off as he considered Lana's words. His forehead scrunched up, then suddenly relaxed. "Wait, I think she did. When Rachel came in to sign a bunch of paperwork, I was showing the guys in the office photos of me and Randy's last rock climb."

"Why on earth would you remember that?"

"Because it was a new route that the others wanted to try out, too. Rachel didn't seem to notice me until our boss told her that Randy had recommended me for a job as guide. Then she did want to take a look. She didn't say anything then about knowing Randy, but after she was finished with the administrative stuff, she asked me out for a drink."

Lana sniggered. "So a sexy stranger ignores you until she hears that you

106

know Randy, but once she does, she asks you out for drinks. Didn't you think it was a little strange?"

Jake grimaced. "When you put it like that, yeah, it was odd. She did ask a lot of questions about Randy during our first date. When I asked why, she said that she'd always enjoyed working with him, but they had lost touch since he had left Straight Up. When I told her about the wedding, she asked if she could be my plus one, but asked to make it a surprise. Honestly, I didn't think it was peculiar at the time. Rachel was hot and came on strong. I was flattered by her attention."

"I can imagine. Rachel had a way of hypnotizing the male species."

"I guess you could call it that, yeah."

"So you booked a ticket to Rome for her without telling Randy. Didn't you think he would mind, especially since he was being so secretive about where the wedding was taking place?"

"He told me he was worried about an ex finding out about the wedding, but I swear he never mentioned her name. Rachel said they were friends from work. I had no reason to suspect her of being Randy's stalker," Jake said resolutely.

As much as she wanted to be mad at him for telling Rachel, Lana understood how the course of events had played out. There was no malicious motivation behind his actions, but simply bad luck.

"Were you following Rachel the night she died, or Randy? I saw you in the city center, close to the Piazza Belvedere, when I was trying to catch up to them."

Her question seemed to throw him momentarily off guard, but he quickly recovered his composure. "No, you must be mistaken. I walked over to the restaurant with Craig, Bruce, and Katherine. Heather showed up later."

"You walked over with Craig?" Lana blurted out.

"He's always so quiet, it's like he disappears into the background. You know what they say about the quiet ones, right? You better watch out for them." Jake winked.

Lana nodded absently, wondering why he was lying again.

"We waited for you until about nine thirty, and when you didn't show,

Katherine did call you," he continued. "But you weren't answering your phone. And when we were walking back to the hotel, we came across that bar."

"Really, Jake? Why can't you tell me the truth? Craig visited a church, by himself, before dinner. He showed me the pictures he'd taken, and I checked the time stamps. His story is true—yours is not. Why did you lie to the police about where you were when Rachel died?"

Jake glared at Lana before letting out a massive sigh. "Alright, so I was following Rachel. But I didn't hurt her! I just wanted to see if she and Randy were a couple or not."

"What do you mean? You landed the babe, as you said before."

Jake puffed out his cheeks. "While I was waiting in the lobby for everyone to return so we could walk over to the restaurant together, Katherine ran inside the hotel and stormed past me. When I looked to see what made her so mad, I saw Rachel waiting outside the hotel. I thought she was waiting for me, so I rose to go to her, but Randy walked outside first."

Jake stopped for a moment, as if he was trying to recall the exact details. "Rachel trailed after him, which meant she was waiting for him, not me. Which made me curious, I will admit. So I followed them."

"Okay, so what happened when you caught up with them?"

"I didn't. I lost sight of her and gave up. So I turned back towards the hotel, and on the way, I spotted a sports bar and had a few beers. That's why I was late to dinner—but not as late as Heather was."

"Why didn't you tell the cops the truth?"

"I got into a couple of scrapes right after college. I had a lot of anger issues and was drinking too much, but I've gotten help since then. I didn't want to bring attention to myself, in case Rachel was murdered. I had nothing to do with it," Jake added quickly, "but the cops might not have looked any further if they saw that I had a police record."

Lana's neck hairs stood on end. "What kind of police record?"

Jake looked down to the floor. "The juvenile kind. Unfortunately, I was stupid enough to get into trouble for youthful transgressions after I'd turned eighteen," he said. "It's been tough enough finding work, as it is. If

I get entangled with the police again, even wrongfully so, it might become impossible."

Lana's eyes narrowed as she scanned his face for signs of deceit. If he lied so easily about his actions, could she trust anything he said?

"You aren't going to tell the others, are you? Heather and Katherine both work at Straight Up Climbs; I can't afford to lose that job," Jake pleaded.

"Alright, I'll keep it to myself," Lana said, adding, "for now" in her mind.

"I saw you and Heather when I was following Rachel, too," Jake pressed. "Heather lied about being at dinner—she didn't show up until after we had already been served dessert. Where was she when Rachel was killed? She did hate her and follows Randy around like a puppy dog. I bet she did it to get rid of her competition—Gloria is probably next. You saw how mean Heather was to her, didn't you?"

Lana forehead crinkled. "What do you mean?"

"Heather is obsessed with Randy! He told me that he's getting sick of her constantly calling to check up on him. I bet she wants to be more than friends, but she's so socially inept that she never figured out how to ask him out."

Lana considered his words. He actually made a good point about Heather, although she doubted that the young woman would actually harm Gloria. Lana made a mental note to talk to Heather about her calls to Randy; however, she was not yet ready to scratch Jake off her suspects list.

Jake took advantage of her hesitation and began walking back towards the others. "I'm going to join the rest, unless you have any more questions?"

"No, we're good," Lana said. She still didn't trust him, and until she spoke to Jeremy and found out more about his background, she probably wouldn't be able to. Lana couldn't wait to see what her friend found out about Jake Segers.

23

Shifting Priorities

After spending two hours absorbing the beauty and history of Saint Peter's Basilica, all of their stomachs were rumbling. Lana led them under the Passetto di Borgo, an aboveground corridor connecting the pontiff's official residence to Castel Sant'Angelo, and towards a busy street running behind the walled city. Towering palms and stone pine trees, their skinny trunks twisting up towards the clear blue sky, lined the sidewalks.

"Hey, Jake, why don't you pick the café?"

He patted his firm stomach. "Happy to oblige." Jake slowed his pace, pausing to read every menu they passed.

The group of friends squeezed onto the busy sidewalk, automatically pairing off. As the euphoria of their visit to the Vatican dissipated, Lana's thoughts turned again to Randy and her investigation. She made a point of stepping in line next to Heather, who appeared to be lost in her thoughts. Lana considered the young woman's motives for harming Rachel, but couldn't really think of anything stronger than protecting Randy. But would she go so far as to kill for him? And if she did, how the heck had she kept it to herself for so long? With her tendency to blurt out every thought, Lana imagined it would be impossible for Heather to keep anything secret.

"Hey Lana," Heather said, seconds later, as if noticing her for the first time. "Have you heard from Randy yet?"

"I'm afraid the police aren't going to let him speak to anyone but his lawyer until he is released. Dotty messaged me when we were in Saint Peter's to let me know that she's found a law firm in Rome willing to represent him. They are sending a lawyer to the police station today."

Heather teared up and looked away, biting her lip in an apparent attempt to control her emotions.

Lana patted her arm. "With a little luck, the lawyer will be able to get Randy released pretty quickly. From what Gloria said, it sounds like their evidence is pretty flimsy."

"I sure hope so." Heather turned to Lana, her gaze intense. "He has already suffered so much because of Rachel. It's not fair that he's being wrongly accused of causing her death, as well."

Lana wondered whether Jake was right and Heather was infatuated with Randy. Would she actually harm Gloria? Lana had to try to find out. "You are a really good friend to Randy."

Heather nodded. "He's the brother I never had."

"And it sounds like it's been an incredibly tough year for him, and his losing his job meant you two haven't seen each other as much as you used to. And now with him marrying Gloria... I bet you miss hanging out with him."

"It's true; he hasn't had as much time for me. But that will change soon enough."

Lana frowned. "What do you mean?"

"Gloria isn't right for him. He needs someone who craves adventures, not having lots of babies," Heather said dismissively. "I bet they don't last a year—well, unless she manages to get pregnant before he can arrange for a divorce."

Lana's eyes widened as she took in the younger woman's proclamation. "Have you ever been in love?"

Heather jutted out her chin. "I don't know if I want to be in a long-term relationship—things can get so messy when others depend on you. I'm happy being alone, and it gives me time to help my friends when they need me. If I was in a relationship, I probably wouldn't have time for them."

Maybe it is better that Randy is putting distance between them, Lana thought. From what Jake had said, Randy was tiring of Heather's constant mothering.

And it sounded like Heather was completely unaware that her behavior was getting on his nerves.

When she noticed Jake pointing towards a tiny bistro and waving them forward, Lana sucked up her breath, knowing it was now or never. "I saw you following Randy the night Rachel died. I even called out to you, but you ran off. Were you trying to protect him or harm Rachel?"

Heather stopped and put her hands on her hips. "Why would I hurt Rachel? If I wanted Randy for myself, it would have been smarter to kill Gloria, don't you think? Besides, I was at dinner with the others when Rachel died," she replied, quite adamantly. "Who says otherwise?"

"Craig and Jake both said that you didn't show up until after the main course had been served."

"Jake is lying again! I don't trust him, Lana," she protested, conveniently not addressing how Craig had made the same observation. "There was something odd going on between Jake and Rachel. He told the police they were dating, but she didn't seem interested in Jake when she was fighting with Randy in the lobby. Didn't Rachel say she flew over to disrupt Randy's wedding and that she and Randy were meant to be together? Rachel must not have loved Jake that much if she flew all the way to Rome to profess her love to another man."

Lana nodded, considering her words. "You make a great point. But I'm more interested in you right now. You don't seem upset by her death in the slightest. What was your beef with her?" Lana said.

"Why should I be sorry that she's gone? Rachel was so bad for Randy. She should have been on that ladder, not him. She finally got what she deserved."

Again with the ladder, Lana thought. Why was Heather was obsessed with that incident? Although, when Lana thought about it, Randy's accident had changed their relationship forever. They no longer worked together and, as a consequence, saw each other far less. Now that he was getting married, his free time would be reduced even further. Randy's fall was a turning point for Heather, Lana realized; it was no wonder that she was fixated on it.

"What do you mean—she got what she deserved? That sounds pretty harsh. You were suspended, too."

Heather froze on the sidewalk as her face began to whiten. "I wasn't suspended..." she began to protest, though halfheartedly.

"According to an article in the *Seattle Chronicle*, you were temporarily suspended right after the accident, along with Rachel."

"Yes, but my suspension was part of the normal investigative procedure because the equipment is my responsibility. Rachel's suspension was unusual in that circumstance. Our boss only took her off the schedule because of Randy's assertions that she was somehow involved."

"Then why did they hire Rachel back?"

"I think Randy is right—Rachel probably was sleeping with one of our managers. She loved to control and manipulate men and used her body as a weapon or prize, depending on the situation. Otherwise I don't know how they could have taken Rachel back, knowing how much pain it would have caused Katherine and me."

Jake jogged back to fetch them. "Hey, guys—we've got a table. Do you want to join us?"

"Sure, thanks. We'll be right there," Lana said brightly.

When Heather sped up, clearly intending to get away from her, Lana grabbed the younger woman's wrist.

"Did you hurt Rachel?" Lana whispered.

"No," Heather hissed, "I did not. But I do applaud whoever did."

24

Channeling Rachel

Jake had chosen well. The Trattoria Vaticano Giggi's selection was mouth-watering, and the café was an open and friendly space, despite being incredibly busy. While they patiently waited for their server to take their order, Lana took in the bright red and yellow walls covered in film-stills of actors eating pasta. Despite the photos encouraging them to order otherwise, they chose an antipasti platter to share.

Lana let her tongue roll over the salty hams, pork, sausages, and salamis, tamed by the freshness of the mozzarella balls, olives, pepperoncini, marinated vegetables, and arugula leaves. The carafes of red wine the waiter had brought over helped to wash away the fat and salt from her palate.

Jake's hunger wasn't sated by the cold cuts, so he ordered a slice of gnocchi potato pie, as well. Although Lana's stomach was far too full to sample it, she made a mental note to try a piece later in the trip. It looked scrumptious, just like the rest of their meal was.

By the time they left the trattoria, all were completely stuffed, so they took two cabs back to the hotel. During lunch, they had unanimously agreed to take a break and rest their feet after they'd wined and dined.

Back in the comfort of her own room, Lana stretched out on her bed and loosened her pants, giving her overly full stomach extra room. *Three suspects down, two to go*, she thought as she stared up at the ceiling. Yet, the remaining pair—Rachel's sister and her brother-in-law—were the least likely to have

114

harmed her, in Lana's mind. Statistically speaking, she knew that people were often murdered by their own family. But in this case, she couldn't see either Bruce or Katherine as being able to do so.

Then again, it must have been someone in this group—or it was Randy, after all. And time was running out for her friend. As implausible as it seemed, she had to consider that Katherine and Bruce were potentially killers.

Lana's beeping phone broke her train of thought. It was a message from Alex. "Arriving early tomorrow morning. Don't worry about picking me up, I'll meet you at the hotel. LOVE YOU!"

As much as his message warmed her heart, it reminded her that she needed to step up her investigation. She had hoped to have a better idea of who could have harmed Rachel by now. When she met up with Randy's friends again tonight, talking to Katherine and Bruce would be her top priority.

They met up in the lobby at 7 p.m. and took two taxis to a restaurant Craig had read about. Its interior was quite industrial, but the food was extraordinarily extravagant and lived up to the glowing reviews the restaurant had received. Despite the delicious meal and unique surroundings, the evening was a bit peculiar thanks to Katherine's metamorphosis.

In a few hours' time, she had transformed herself into a Rachel-lite. It was unsettling to see Katherine wearing her dead sister's shoes, clothes, and makeup. Gone were the muted browns and grays that she normally favored; instead, she was wearing a pink and green ensemble that was so bright it hurt Lana's eyes. When she moved, the multitudes of rings, armbands, and necklaces that she now wore shimmered and jangled. Even stranger was her newly found self-assurance. It was as if Katherine was channeling Rachel's personality as well, because she was no longer a wallflower, but a temptress.

Bruce seemed to be freaked out by the transformation, as well. He kept an eye on his girlfriend throughout the meal, his brows raised in astonishment as she flirted openly with the waitstaff and even slapped the sommelier's backside after he delivered their wine.

The rest of their friends clearly noticed Katherine's makeover, yet none dared to ask her about it directly. Luckily, they had enough to chat about to keep the conversation rolling throughout the dinner. After a scrumptious meal of tender lamb, baby potatoes with rosemary, and delicately grilled vegetables, Lana was satisfied, happy, and up for anything.

"What should we do now?" Bruce asked.

"Go to a bar?" Craig asked.

"Shouldn't we call Randy or Gloria and see if we can do anything to help him first?" Heather pushed. "I called them both when we were taking a break, but neither has gotten back to me."

"What can we do that the police cannot?" Craig retorted.

"We have to be patient," Lana said. "Randy's lawyer should be there by now. I'm certain the police will release him quite soon."

Katherine pushed back her chair and rose. "Then let's go out and celebrate for Randy."

When they passed a bar with dance music blaring out of the windows, Katherine clapped her hands and began shaking her hips in time with the rhythm. "I love this song!" she exclaimed before rushing inside.

"You do?" Bruce asked as he trailed after her.

Lana watched in wonder. Their dynamic today was quite different than what she was used to. *What happened during our short break to warrant such a drastic change?* she wondered.

Once they were inside, Katherine took off another layer of clothes, exposing a tank top that left little to the imagination, and tossed it at Bruce. Still, no one dared to ask her about her metamorphosis. Thinking it may have something to do with Rachel's demise, Lana decided to take the plunge.

"Hey, Katherine. Wow, I've never seen you wear such colorful clothes before. They suit you."

Katherine sashayed her way over to Lana and grabbed her hands, twirling her once, before releasing her. "They were Rachel's. The police brought over her belongings this morning and left them for me at the reception desk. Seeing as she won't need them anymore, I figured I'd try out some of her clothes. They are a lot brighter than I usually wear, but I like the way they make me feel," she cooed as she ran her hands over her silky skirt. "I feel like a vixen in these—no wonder Rachel could land any man she wanted to. I'm going to go have some fun. Care to join me, Bruce?"

Bruce flushed bright pink and looked to the ground.

Katherine shrugged. "Suit yourself," she muttered before disappearing into the crowded dance floor.

What was going on with those two? It was as if their personalities had switched. Katherine's decision to wear her dead sister's wardrobe was creepy, but perhaps that was her way of coping. She was so much more confident now than Lana had ever seen her. In one sense, it was a good sign, but the reason behind the change did concern her. Was it a healthy reaction?

Lana moved closer to Bruce. He looked so stricken. She followed his gaze to see why. Katherine was flirting with a stranger while stealing coy glances at Bruce. Bruce, in turn, stared at his girlfriend, yet didn't move in to claim his territory.

"Grief does weird things to a person," Lana said as they watched the stranger buying Katherine a drink.

"She's on an emotional roller coaster, I think. One minute she's trying to come to terms with having to work with Rachel again, and the next minute she has to tell her parents that their favorite daughter is dead."

"How did they take it?"

"As well as you could expect, I guess. Luckily the police had called them before Katherine did, so they were already getting used to the shocking news. Her mother is inconsolable, but her father was calmer."

"If there's anything I can do..."

"That's what you're supposed to say, isn't it?" Bruce's sad smile almost broke her heart. They both turned to Katherine, now twirling on the dance floor with yet another male patron.

"Katherine really didn't know that Rachel was coming back to work?"

Bruce shook his head. "She had no idea. I cannot believe none of the managers told her. They all knew that those two didn't get along. But Rachel did have a way of wrapping men around her finger. I bet she asked whoever hired her back not to."

"How is it that you all live in the same city and never see each other?"

"Katherine's parents don't invite us over often, and when they do, it's usually for one of their big parties. They like to invite hundreds of people, so it's easy for us to avoid Rachel when we're there."

"I don't understand why she and Katherine disliked each other so much."

"Rachel did everything she could to humiliate and belittle Katherine. I'm sorry she's dead, but I am glad she can't hurt Katherine anymore. If only her parents will let her in. I'm a little worried her mom is going to bury herself in her charities and pretend like Katherine doesn't exist."

"How heartbreaking," Lana said sympathetically. She gazed over at Katherine, now with her arms around another man's neck. "Not to be a jerk, but you two don't seem to be as lovey dovey as you were before Rachel passed away. Did you two get into a fight, as well?"

"Are you serious? Look at her." Katherine was climbing onto a table with the help of her new male friend. Moments later, she began dancing provocatively for a cheering crowd.

"I didn't even know she could dance. She always said she had two left feet." To Lana, Bruce looked concerned, and a touch scared.

"She's become a totally different person in a few hours' time. As soon as we got Rachel's suitcases up to the room, she tore them open and began trying everything on. She's never been interested in fashion, makeup, or jewelry before. And as soon as she put on Rachel's clothes, her personality seemed to transform, in a nasty way. I don't know if it's pent-up grief or jealousy, but it's scaring me. I want my girlfriend back."

As if called, Katherine sprung off the table and rushed over to them before grabbing Bruce and kissing him passionately.

Bruce pulled back from her embrace, clearly stunned.

Katherine laughed. "What's wrong? I thought you liked women to take control!" She shot him a wicked smile, then sashayed her way back to the dance floor. Self-confidence oozed off of her.

"Do you think she hurt Rachel?" Lana asked.

"I want to say no, that Katherine could never have hurt her sister, but I really don't know what to think right now. I've never seen her like this," he said, his eyes never leaving his girlfriend.

As Lana watched him watching Katherine, a thought sprung into her mind. "Bruce, were you and Rachel ever romantically involved?"

His head whipped around. "Why would you think that?"

"Because Rachel seemed to have flirted with—or dated—pretty much every male who came within her vicinity."

He ran his hands over his face. "You're right about that—Rachel saw every man she met as a potential suitor. I am not proud of it, but Rachel and I did kiss once at a party. I was drunk and obviously not thinking clearly because Katherine is the best thing that's ever happened to me."

"Does Katherine know?"

"No!' Bruce grabbed Lana's shoulders and turned her so he could look her in the eye. "I shouldn't have said anything to you. Please, I don't know what the truth would do to her. She was so worried about me and Rachel meeting because her sister tended to steal her boyfriends away, then dump them soon after."

Lana frowned up at him. "So why did you kiss Rachel if you knew what it would do to your girlfriend?"

Bruce released his grip and looked away. "When I first met Rachel, I didn't understand why Katherine was so concerned. She was kind, considerate, and didn't seem to be interested in me whatsoever. But a few months later, we were all at a mutual friend's birthday party, and Rachel cornered me. Katherine had a headache and had left early, but I wanted to stay a bit longer. Rachel was so flattering and funny, and she kept bringing me more beers. Before I knew it, she was leading me to a back room, and we were on a bed, kissing. It's like she had hypnotized me."

"How could you, Bruce? Poor Katherine. I can imagine she would be extremely upset if she found out. Did you sleep with Rachel?"

"No way! That was the creepy part. She pushed me onto the bed and told me how she could make me so much happier than Katherine ever could. It sobered me right up. It was pretty clear that she was only kissing me to hurt her sister. Ever since then, I've avoided Rachel at all costs. Katherine means so much to me; I don't want to lose her."

"What do you think she would do, if she ever found out?"

"Scratch Rachel's eyes out for starters," Bruce responded and then paled. "I didn't mean that literally. No matter how strangely Kat is acting, she would never have hurt her own sister. She simply isn't capable of it."

"No, of course not," Lana soothed. Yet she couldn't help but wonder what the truth would have done to Katherine. Was grief making her act so strangely? Or was jealousy driving her mad? Lana had to find out more about the sisters' fight she had witnessed from her hotel room.

"You aren't going to say anything to Katherine, are you? Seeing as how Rachel's dead, there's no reason to come clean."

"I guess you're right." Lana watched Katherine down another drink before springing back onto the table. Bruce had enough on his hands to worry about right now. Besides, she was more concerned about Randy's freedom than the future of Katherine's relationship.

25

Emerging From the Shadows

December 20—Day Three of the Wanderlust Tour in Rome, Italy

Heather and Katherine walked arm in arm on their way back to the hotel, giggling and singing as they stumbled across the center of Rome. The rest trailed after them, though in a less exuberant fashion. Lana considered cornering Katherine and trying to find out more about her fight with Rachel, but she quickly ditched the idea. Katherine was far too drunk to talk coherently. She had been receiving free drinks all night, and Bruce had to fight off one of her admirers when they wanted to leave.

The next morning, Katherine was downstairs in the breakfast hall, nursing a coffee and a hangover, when Lana entered the room. She scurried over and sat down across from Katherine, seizing her chance to chat freely before the others arrived.

"Hey, how are you holding up?"

Katherine grimaced and held her head. "I don't know what came over me. I never drink that much. I don't know if it was the clothes, jewelry, or music, but it was like I was possessed by my sister. It scares me a little because I liked it," she whispered, staring at Lana with red-rimmed eyes. "What does that say about me? I despised Rachel."

Lana laid a hand over hers. "Oh, hon, you two may not have gotten along, but she was your sister. Like it or not, you do share the same set of genes."

Katherine blinked back a tear. "I wish my parents thought the same way. I wasn't as perfect as Rachel, but I deserve their love, too."

She took a swig of her coffee as Lana struggled to think of the right thing to say. Before she could, Katherine continued.

"Part of me is glad that she's gone. And that's what's making me crazy. You're not supposed to be happy when your sibling dies, are you?"

"No, I guess not," Lana admitted. "But it's not like you two had a healthy relationship."

"I wouldn't have hurt her, but it is freeing, knowing she is gone," Katherine added. "Did you know that my parents introduce us as Rachel and her sister? Can you imagine how humiliating that is? For the first time, I'm not 'the sister of'—I'm just Katherine."

Lana could feel her eyes welling up. How could Katherine's parents treat her so cruelly? "Are they doing alright?"

"I have no idea—Mom hasn't returned any of my calls."

"I'm so sorry. Maybe they'll come around once they've had time to digest this news."

"They have spent the past twenty-five years pretending I don't exist. I doubt that will change."

"At least you have Bruce."

Katherine laughed bitterly. "That's not really a consolation right now."

"What is going on between you two—did you have a fight?"

Katherine bit her lip as she looked away. "No, we didn't. I'm not good with confrontations, but it might be cathartic if we did."

"I saw you and Rachel fighting outside of our hotel after she and Randy had that argument in the lobby. What were you two arguing about?"

"What are you talking about? I didn't see her after she stormed out of our hotel."

Lana's eyebrows furrowed. "That's not true—I saw you two fighting outside of the hotel a few minutes before Randy left for the train station."

When Katherine began shaking her head no, Lana added, "I saw you slap Rachel. Please don't deny it."

Katherine's eyes narrowed momentarily before her shoulders slumped.

"What does it matter now? Rachel is dead; she can't hurt me anymore."

Lana sucked in her breath. "Were you afraid that she was going to steal Bruce away? Is that why you hit her?"

"Yes." Katherine's voice cracked. "When you saw us fighting on the sidewalk, she had just told me about her and Bruce kissing at a party and how little it would take to steal him away. It really hurt to hear that he'd done that to me, but I know it wasn't his fault. Rachel seduced him, just like she did all of my other boyfriends. She had to have him because he was mine. It was just a game to her. I wanted to kill her."

"Did you?"

"No, I slapped her instead. I couldn't have truly hurt her even if I'd wanted to. We were sisters." Katherine sighed. "Now that she is gone, Bruce is all mine. I'm just not sure if I want him."

"Don't say that! You two are great together. Please don't make any rash decisions right now. Give yourself time to adjust to Rachel's death."

Katherine ignored Lana's remarks, instead choosing to down her coffee.

"Why do you think she was so obsessed with Randy? I mean, Rachel seemed like the kind of girl who could have gotten any man she pleased. Why did she focus all of her attention on the one who wasn't interested in her?"

Katherine pursed her lips. "Precisely for that reason. Most men would have done anything to be with Rachel. She'd received countless marriage proposals, but laughed them all off. Rachel wasn't interested in having a healthy, loving relationship. She wanted to be in control and manipulate others, and she was certainly not interested in being tied down to one man. I honestly don't think Rachel knew what real love was."

She rose, signaling the end of their conversation. Lana didn't push. When Katherine grabbed her cup off the table and turned away, the door to the breakfast hall burst open.

"There you are!" Bruce called across the room, alarm in his voice.

"Speak of the devil..." Katherine murmured.

He ran over to her. "I was so worried when I woke up and saw you were gone." He went to wrap her up in a hug, but Katherine stiffened and stepped away.

"Sorry, I need a little space this morning. My head is killing me."

Bruce looked like a scolded puppy dog. "Oh, okay." He started to turn away when he noticed the empty coffee cup in her hand. "Can I get you a refill?"

Katherine startled but handed him the mug. "Sure, that would be great."

"When I get back, could I massage your shoulders? I know that helps with your headaches."

Her expression softened as she tentatively took his hand. "I would love that. Thank you."

Bruce pulled her hand to his lips, kissing it softly. "Anything for you, my love."

Lana smiled at the young couple, glad to see they hadn't shut each other out completely. There was hope for them yet.

26

Alex to the Rescue

When the breakfast room door opened again, a familiar voice called out, "Lana!"

"Alex! Boy, I sure missed you. How are you doing, darling?" Lana asked as she fell into his arms.

"Better now," he said, nuzzling her neck.

"Hey, Alex!" Bruce waved them over to his table, where Alex shook his hand and pecked Katherine on one cheek.

"You hanging in there?" Bruce asked.

Alex ran a hand through his wavy hair. "I guess. I'm really worried about Randy. The police don't seem to be searching for other suspects."

Lana took his hand and threaded her fingers through his. "What did your boss say?"

"He is going to cover my sessions so I won't lose my job."

"Thank goodness!"

Alex looked to Bruce and Katherine. "Do you mind if I steal Lana away for a few minutes?"

"Of course, take all the time you need. We'll wait for you down here," Bruce said with a wink.

Once they were back in Lana's hotel room, Alex sat down heavily on the bed, pulling her down next to him. "I missed you so much. But despite what Bruce thinks, I am not feeling romantically inclined right now. I can't stop thinking about Randy."

"I understand completely," Lana said and kissed him on the forehead.

"What have you found out so far?"

"Nothing that indicates one of them had a strong motive for murdering Rachel, I'm afraid." Lana puffed out her cheeks. "It's such a strange idea, investigating Randy's friends like this. Deep down, I hope that it wasn't one of them, but a stranger, who did this."

"I understand completely. Randy's known all of them for years, well, except for Jake. It's hard to believe any of them could do this. Yet, the police maintain the person who harmed Rachel was wearing a Straight Up Climbs jacket," Alex said.

"What if Randy did pull Rachel away from that hotel's awning, but someone else killed her?" Lana reasoned.

"Then we are out of luck. Besides, Randy says he didn't see her during his walk to the station. As strange as it sounds, we better hope one of his friends did it, if we want to set him free," Alex said grimly. "Otherwise we're probably never going to know who did this."

He took her hand and kissed her fingertips. "I need to know what you've found out. Someone hurt Rachel, and I refuse to believe it was my baby brother."

Lana pulled away from her boyfriend and sat up straighter, determined to tell him everything. "For starters, I don't think Craig could have done it. He was in a church at the time, on the other side of town from where Rachel was killed. I saw the pictures he took and checked the time stamps."

Alex frowned. "I doubt Craig would have had a motive to hurt Rachel. As far as I know, they barely knew each other."

"Apparently they knew each other quite well. Believe it or not, Craig said that he and Rachel went out a few times after Randy broke up with her. But he thinks it was so she could keep tabs on Randy. She dumped him pretty fast, once Craig stopped sharing information about Randy with her."

"Ouch. Being used like that must have hurt."

"It must not have bruised his ego too badly because they recently met up in a bar and talked long enough for him to tell her about Randy's wedding."

"What!" Alex's face clouded over. "So he is the reason why Rachel knew where the wedding was taking place. I can't believe it. Craig is one of Randy's oldest friends."

"I am afraid he wasn't the first one to inform her. Craig said she already knew it was taking place in Italy on December 24. During our interview with the police, Jake told the officers that he and Rachel were dating. When I confronted him about it, Jake admitted that he had told Rachel."

"Does friendship hold no meaning anymore? How could Jake do that to Randy?"

"He claims that he didn't know Randy and Rachel had ever dated, and I have to say that I believe him. I've known Randy for a year now and never heard of Rachel or of him having had a stalker before."

"Whether Jake meant to betray Randy or not—he did tell Rachel. If he had kept his mouth shut, Randy would be in Il Pino with Gloria right now instead of in a jail cell. I can't believe Craig blabbed, as well! I'll deal with them both later. Who is next?"

"Wait—Il Pino? Is that where Gloria's grandfather's vineyard is?"

"Yes."

Lana cocked an eyebrow at him. "You knew the name of the mystery village the whole time?"

Alex held up his hands. "Randy's secret, not mine. He was desperate to keep it under wraps so he only told those who needed to know. And with reason, it seems. Who's next on your suspect list?"

"Bruce. He doesn't seem the murdering type, either. And I don't think he had enough of a motive to actually want to kill Rachel."

"Did he have any motive? Rachel is his girlfriend's older sister, so technically they are practically family."

"Bruce and Rachel kissed at a party long ago, and he is terrified that Katherine will find out about it."

"Geez, I would have thought his girlfriend's sister would have been off-limits."

"He claims Rachel seduced him when he was inebriated, otherwise he would have fended her off. But it doesn't really matter; he and Katherine

127

were at dinner when Rachel was killed. Their waiter even took a picture of them. Based on the time stamp, they would not have had enough time to get to the Trevi and back again. At least, not without anyone noticing."

"I bet Katherine would go through the roof if she ever found out about it. If Bruce was afraid she would leave him if Rachel told her, he might have thought that silencing her was the only way to save his relationship."

"If he did, he wasted his time. Katherine already knew. A few minutes before Randy left for the train station, Katherine and Rachel got into an argument outside of the hotel. Rachel gloated about their kiss and threatened to steal Bruce away."

"Man, Rachel was so mean to her. But did Bruce know that Rachel had already told Katherine?" Alex asked.

"Good question. That's worth checking out. Yet as mad as Katherine is about Rachel and Bruce, I can't believe she would have killed her sister. She's too meek for starters. However, she has been acting strange since Rachel died, and I don't know if the cause is guilt or grief."

"That photograph proves they were both at the restaurant at that moment, but maybe one or both left and came back? From what Randy has told me, Katherine has been living in Rachel's shadow since birth. Maybe she saw her chance to get rid of her sister, once and for all?"

"I guess we could ask the waitstaff if they remember Katherine or Bruce leaving for a half hour," Lana said carefully. It was a long shot, but she understood his desire to identify another potential killer, if only to encourage the police to keep looking for other suspects.

"That leaves Jake or Heather."

Lana nodded. "They both lied to me and the cops about where they were when Rachel died. I saw them when I was trailing after Randy, and I swear they seemed to be following him, too. But I lost them, just as I did Randy and Rachel. Craig said Jake and Heather showed up late for dinner, which means both were probably in the vicinity of the Trevi when Rachel died, so they could have done it. I don't know if that means they are involved with the murder, but it is suspicious."

"Have you asked either one about it?"

"I did. Jake denied it at first, but finally broke down and told me that he was trailing after Rachel. He claims he lied to the cops about it because he didn't want them to check out his background. He's been in trouble with the law before, but he was vague about what he'd done. I've already asked Jeremy to look into it."

"Jeremy is a great guy. If there is anything to be found, he'll find it. And Heather?"

"She is adamant that she was at that dinner, but the rest have made clear that she didn't show up until after dessert was served. And I saw her right before I reached the Trevi Fountain. I even called out her name, but she took off running when she looked back and saw me."

"That sounds quite suspicious. It might be important to know what she was doing when you saw her. But I can't imagine Heather hurting Rachel, no matter how much she disliked her. However, there is only one way to be certain—let's talk to her," Alex said as he stood up. Lana pulled him gently back down onto the bed.

"Before we do, I have a few questions about Heather." Lana was silent a moment, wondering how to broach this next subject. Heather's reactions to Rachel's arrival and Randy's arrest had brought a wild idea into her mind, but she was almost afraid to ask Alex about it. She had to tread lightly; Heather was an old family friend, after all.

"This entire trip Heather has been beating herself up about that ladder and how Rachel should have been on it, not Randy. What can you tell me about the accident?"

"Why do you ask?"

"Do you remember anything strange about it?"

"The whole thing was strange!" Alex exploded. "I'm sorry. I feel so helpless and want to do everything I can to help my brother, but I don't think his mountain-climbing accident has anything to do with Rachel's death."

"I'm not so sure," Lana said.

"Personally, I think the ladder was faulty," Alex said. "It's not unheard of for a piece of equipment to fail, especially one that's a few years old. In fact, Randy's fall wasn't that bad because the ladder collapsed as soon as he put his weight on it. If his leg hadn't gotten caught up in the rungs, then he would have dusted himself off and kept on working."

His response encouraged Lana to push forward with her theory. "Why do you think Randy is convinced that Rachel was behind it?"

Alex grimaced and blew out his cheeks. "I love my brother, but Rachel's stalking was making him extremely paranoid. In that sense, I can understand why he blamed her for his accident at the time. But I don't think she had anything to do with it. It was just bad luck."

"Okay, that makes sense. But was there anything odd about Heather's reaction to his accident?"

"She took it really hard, almost like she'd let Randy down somehow. But then again, maintaining their equipment is her responsibility, and his ladder did fail. You know, now that you mention it, I always wondered if she had forgotten to check the latch and felt guilty about it."

Lana's eyes widened as she realized what this could mean for Randy. "But no one accused her of negligence?"

"Not as far as I know. The insurance company tested every piece of gear they had after that and couldn't find a single thing wrong. Frankly, I think that's what saved Heather's job. If they had found more equipment that wasn't in top condition, the resulting lawsuits might have been the end of both her career and Straight Up Climbs. But because the incident was officially declared an accident, Randy wasn't able to sue anyone."

"Was he trying to?"

"Randy wasn't interested in pursuing a lawsuit, but our parents were pushing hard for him to do so. Straight Up's insurance paid for a lot of his medical care, but not all of it. Randy had to borrow money from our parents to pay all of his hospital bills and the rehabilitation, and they were hoping for some financial relief, I think," Alex said in a sheepish voice.

"Wait a second—Rachel was supposed to place the ladder that day, right? I take it Heather would have gotten her gear ready for her?"

"Yeah, I guess. That is Heather's job."

"But Rachel suddenly gets sick and has to leave at the last minute. And Randy was the one who volunteered to take her place."

Alex looked at her, puzzled. "As far as I know, that's what happened. Where are you going with this?"

"What would have happened if the ladder had collapsed while Randy was out over the crevasse?"

"He would definitely have been more seriously injured and possibly have died," Alex said resolutely.

Lana groaned. "Of course! Rachel was a lot lighter than Randy. After I told everyone that Rachel was dead, Heather made a really callous comment about how she finally got what she deserved."

Alex looked at her, puzzled. "What does that have to do with—" His eyes widened as his thoughts aligned with Lana's. "You don't really think..."

"That Heather intentionally sabotaged that ladder in the hopes that Rachel would get injured? Yes, that is exactly what I'm thinking may have happened."

"But why? I mean, she and Randy were always close, but never romantically involved."

"Heather did know how much Rachel was messing up Randy's life. All she would have had to do was bend that clasp enough so it wouldn't hold completely. Randy is heavier than Rachel, so the ladder collapsed immediately. Considering how thin Rachel was, she may have been able to make it halfway across before it failed. And from what you've told me, it would have been a far more serious accident."

Alex shook his head. "Okay, even if that is true—which is a long shot—why would Heather have killed Rachel?"

"To finish off the job."

Alex shook his head adamantly. "You're crazy. Heather would never harm another soul. I've known her all my life. She doesn't have it in her, Lana."

"Did you know she'd been arrested for inciting violence during a protest—twice? I found a photo of her in the local paper biting a police officer."

Alex gritted his teeth. "Oh, I knew she'd been arrested, but I didn't know what for."

"Rachel was stalking Randy, and even after he threatened to go to the police, she kept at it. Randy would have told Heather about it—they were good friends and worked together. What if Heather saw her chance to get rid of Rachel by sabotaging her gear? But it didn't work; instead, her actions put Randy in the hospital and cost him his job."

Lana sprung up and began pacing as her theory began to take flight. "Then Rachel showed up here in Rome and threatened Randy again. What if she drowned Rachel in order to protect Randy? Think about it, Alex. In a sick way, that would be the ultimate display of friendship."

"For a psychopath maybe," Alex said with a frown. "No, I can't see that happening."

"There's only one way to find out. We ask her."

"Do you really think she is going to tell you the truth?"

"Heather wears her heart on her sleeve. If we confront her directly about it, I bet it will be impossible for her to lie. You two have known each other for years."

Alex opened his mouth to protest, but then shrugged, evidently having changed his mind. "Okay, you win. We'll talk to her about it. Say, did Dotty send you the name of Randy's lawyer?"

"Yes, she did. I have his email address and telephone number, too."

Alex stood up and kissed her forehead. "You're a lifesaver. Let me call the lawyer and see where he's at. I doubt he's been able to do much so far, but I need to know. Then we can talk to Heather and Jake. Though I doubt they are going to tell us anything new."

"I don't know," Lana responded, making her tone as light as possible. "Even if Heather didn't hurt Rachel, she may have seen something suspicious. It's worth a shot."

27

The Best Intentions

"Hey, Alex. It's great to see you," Heather said, as she leaned forward on her toes and gave him a peck on the cheek.

"You, too," he replied warmly. "Sorry I haven't had time to catch up with you yet. Randy being arrested is not exactly how I envisioned that this week would go."

Heather blinked back tears. "I know. I can't stop thinking about him. It's not fair—Randy doesn't deserve to be locked up."

She broke down into sobs, and Alex took her in his arms and rocked her gently.

Lana could imagine having to interrogate his brother's longtime friend was incredibly painful for him. But in order to help Randy, they needed to know why Heather was lying. Lana was not convinced that she was involved with Rachel's death, but at this point, grasping at straws was better than sitting around doing nothing.

When Heather's sniffles subsided, she patted Alex's shoulder and stepped out of his embrace. "How are you doing? Have you talked to Randy since he was taken into custody?"

Alex shook his head. "I'm afraid the police aren't letting any of us talk to him directly. His lawyer is going to try to get some of their evidence dismissed, but the police are dragging their feet with everything. He thinks it's because they don't have another suspect. And from what they've told him, it doesn't sound like the police are actively searching for one, either."

He paused and looked to Lana, a pleading expression on his face.

He can't do it, she realized before nodding subtly. They had agreed before walking up to Heather's room that he should ask her the questions. Alex had known her far longer, and they had a better bond than she and Lana did. But now that he was faced with having to actually interrogate his brother's longtime friend, he couldn't go through with it.

"Heather, honey, we know how much you care about Randy," Lana said. "Since the police aren't really doing much to help him, we are trying to find out more about what happened to Rachel that night. I saw her trailing after Randy when he left the hotel, so I ran after them to try to warn him. But I kept losing sight of them. However, I did see you when I was a block or so away from the Trevi. Did you see anyone try to talk to either Randy or Rachel, or get their attention somehow?"

"I wasn't following him!" Heather cried.

"You had your Straight Up Climbs jacket on, and you turned around when I called out your name," Lana stated, her tone gentle, yet firm.

"It wasn't me!"

"Heather, stop lying," Alex pleaded. "We need to know what happened that night. What did you see? Did anyone approach Rachel to try to get her attention? Help us set Randy free."

Heather shook her head violently, but one look at Alex's face made her stop and tear up again. "I'm so sorry, Alex. You're right. After Rachel died, I didn't want the police to know I was following them because I was worried they might think I was somehow involved. But I wasn't—I didn't hurt her! I kept losing sight of them, too."

She sucked up her breath before blurting out, "I was following Randy. The hotel bar didn't have the mineral water that I like, so I sat down next to the entrance to people watch while I waited for everyone else to come back down so we could go to dinner. All of a sudden, Katherine stormed inside, madder than I've ever seen her. Then Jake rushed right past me and ran outside. So I went to take a look, and I saw Randy, Rachel, and Jake all walking away. I was worried Rachel was going to try to provoke Randy again and was concerned he might overreact. So I went after them. I wanted to be there, in case he needed help."

"What did you think you could do to help him?" Lana asked.

Heather glared at her. "I was trying to protect Randy from Rachel. If she had confronted him again, I'm not sure what he would have done to her."

"Are you in love with Randy? Is that what this is all about?" Lana asked. "You do seem against him and Gloria getting married."

"No! I wanted to keep him safe. Randy is the brother I never had; I would do anything for him. But I don't want to marry him. I don't really want to marry anyone."

"Did you see anything strange when you were following them through the city?" Alex asked, refocusing Heather's attention on the night Rachel died.

"As soon as I rounded the first street corner, I saw Lana following Randy, too. That was pretty strange to see all of us trailing after him like that. From what I could see, he was oblivious to our presence; he was talking on the phone and didn't look behind him once. He's taller than me and walks a whole lot faster. Every time I got close enough to yell out, he crossed over a busy street or turned a corner and didn't seem to hear me."

"Did anyone else try to talk to him—maybe one of those kids selling tickets, a café owner calling him over to look at the menu, or a lost tourist?" Alex asked. From his tone, Lana could tell he was feeling increasingly despondent.

"No, I didn't see anyone approach him or Rachel. All I wanted to do was protect him from her, but it backfired again. I lost sight of them before Randy reached the train station and didn't find either one of them inside."

Lana shot Alex a knowing look and saw that he was staring at Heather as if he had never seen her before.

"What do you mean—it backfired again?" asked Alex.

Heather began to tremble.

"Randy's ladder," Lana whispered. "You bent the latch and caused his fall, didn't you?"

Heather's eyes welled up with tears. "I feel so ashamed. He wasn't supposed to get hurt—Rachel was. It is my fault he lost his job," she admitted. "I just wanted Rachel to leave him alone. That woman was like poison."

Alex stared at her in horror. "I can't believe it. You bent the safety catch?"

"Rachel was supposed to be on that ladder—not Randy! I would never have hurt him intentionally," she sobbed.

"You destroyed his life!"

"I didn't mean to! I just wanted Rachel to leave him be. I was so mad when he told me about her stalking him. I wanted to scare her so she would quit—I wasn't trying to kill her."

"How could you do that, and not tell anyone?"

Heather stared up at Alex as if he was crazy. "I caused the worst accident in my best friend's life. His blaming Rachel was a blessing at the time, but the guilt has been eating at me ever since. And when Rachel showed up here and threatened to ruin his wedding, I thought if I could keep her away from him, it would somehow make up for the pain I'd caused him."

Lana finally understood why Heather was so concerned with Randy. Her obsession was not driven by a romantic interest, but by guilt.

When Lana and Alex remained silent, Heather added, "You know I would do anything to help Randy, but I didn't kill Rachel! I wish I could tell you who did, but I cannot."

Lane felt a rush of sympathy for the young woman. She had unintentionally destroyed her friend's career and health, in her bizarre attempt to help him. Lana could only imagine the depth of the pain Heather had been feeling this past year, especially since Randy was no longer a part of her daily life.

Alex, on the other hand, was clearly disgusted with Heather and her actions. "Whether you meant to or not, you destroyed his life. I want you to leave Randy alone. Don't ruin his marriage with Gloria—she is the one who has truly helped him, not you. If you really care about Randy, you'll never contact him again."

Heather fell onto her bed and broke down in tears. Alex's face remained impassive as he crossed to the door and exited without looking back.

Lana was less inclined to cast Heather aside, yet she didn't want to upset her boyfriend further by taking the younger woman's side right now. "Alex doesn't mean it; he's just extremely upset and worried for his brother."

"It doesn't matter—once Alex tells Randy about what I did, he won't want

136

me to be in his life anymore," Heather whimpered.

Lana shrugged. "I'm not so sure. Randy's got a heart of gold—he might be able to look past this, one day. But I think Alex is right; it might be best if you left the Wright brothers alone for the time being. Assuming we can get Randy out of jail."

Heather's sniffles increased in volume. However, Lana was not really interested in consoling her. Like Alex, she was having difficulty stomaching the fact that Heather had gone so far as to sabotage a coworker's gear, even if it was out of a misguided attempt to help a friend.

28

One Nasty Character

"I cannot believe this. Heather and Randy have been friends for as long as I can remember. How could she do that to him?" Alex raged, his pent-up frustration and feelings of helplessness bubbling to the surface.

"But she didn't do it *to* Randy, she did it *for* Randy," Lana soothed. When Alex shot her a confused and hurt look, she added, "As twisted as it is, she sabotaged the ladder because she wanted Rachel out of Randy's life. If she had known Randy would end up climbing it, she never would have done it."

Alex froze momentarily before nodding slightly. "Okay, I see your point. But endangering another to help a friend is not a normal reaction! She could have killed Rachel. And how the heck did she keep it a secret for so long?"

"Heather may be a blabbermouth, but even she must have known that if Randy found out, that would be the end of their friendship. You're right; Randy wouldn't have approved of Heather harming Rachel, no matter what the reason."

"What if Heather saw her chance to push Rachel into the Trevi and took it?" Alex sprung up and began pacing in front of their bed. "She did tamper with the ladder, so she's cold-hearted enough to actually go through with it. Those surveillance camera images are usually grainy, and you said it was raining really hard, so visibility would have been worse than normal. I bet the police couldn't see Randy's face and just identified him based on that jacket. And Heather was wearing hers, as well."

Lana nodded in agreement. "That was my initial reaction, as well. But the more I think about it, the more I wonder if Heather is capable of murdering someone in such a personal way."

"She tried to kill Rachel before."

"Tampering with a guide's equipment is vastly different than drowning someone—the latter is much more hands on. Is Heather truly vicious enough to have attacked her like that? And is she strong enough? Heather is far more petite than Rachel was."

Alex opened his mouth to respond, but Lana's phone began ringing. "It's Jeremy. I better take this."

She answered and immediately put the call on speaker. "Hey, there. I didn't expect to hear from you so soon."

"Lana! What I found out can't wait. That Jake Segers guy sounds pretty nasty. Are he and Randy really friends?"

Lana's ears perked up as Alex moved in closer. "What kind of guy is he?"

"The kind that likes to hit women. He was kicked out of college because he pushed his girlfriend down a flight of stairs during a university party. She broke her arm and leg."

Lana sank onto the bed, and Alex followed suit.

"She pressed charges but dropped them after he was kicked out of college," Jeremy explained. "Her parents did win a civil court case against him, so he had to pay for her medical expenses. After that, he moved away from Oregon and worked a bunch of odd jobs. He didn't attend college again, but was arrested and convicted for two counts of assault and battery—first in Illinois and later in South Carolina."

"Oh, lordy. Did your reporters find out any of the details?"

"In Chicago, he was working as security at a nightclub and got grabby with a female patron. When she slapped him with her purse, he punched her in the jaw and broke it in two places. The second incident happened in Charleston; his date refused his advances, so he smashed a wine bottle over her head. And in a crowded restaurant, to boot."

"That is sickening. He seems so normal, I can hardly believe it." Chills went up Lana's spine. She would have never guessed from his behavior on this trip that Jake was capable of harming others so easily.

"He was ordered by a court to attend alcohol abuse and anger management therapy classes after the second incident. My reporters couldn't find any more references to him being in legal trouble after that. Which makes sense, given the three-strikes law."

Alex raised an eyebrow at her.

"That's right—the three-strikes-you're-out rule means if he gets arrested again, the next sentence would automatically be life imprisonment," Lana replied, for Alex's sake. "That is definitely a good reason to stay out of trouble."

"Does he come across as hot-tempered now? That last incident was four years ago. Maybe he has learned to control his anger," Jeremy mused.

Lana thought on Craig and Jake's squabbling. When Craig had degraded and belittled him, Jake had kept his cool and hadn't responded verbally or physically.

"He's fairly zen, actually. Maybe the classes did help," Lana responded as she mulled this information over. "Thanks, Jeremy. It is definitely worth talking to him about all of this and seeing what he has to say for himself."

"Lana, this guy sounds volatile. Maybe he has changed, but it still scares me, you being there with him. Especially if he knows you are trying to figure out who really killed Rachel. If he is involved with her death, he might lash out at you. Promise me you won't confront him alone."

"Don't you worry—the last thing I want to do is get cornered by a killer." She smiled up at her boyfriend, who was watching her closely as he listened in to their conversation. "Alex just arrived from Portugal. I'll make sure he goes with me."

"And I'm happy to do so," Alex said as he squeezed her shoulder.

"Great to hear your voice, Alex," Jeremy said. "I hope this information helps you two get Randy released."

"Me, too."

"Hey, before I go, there's something else you two need to know," Jeremy said.

"Okay, shoot," Lana said.

"I asked one of my crime reporters to check out Rachel Merriweather, as well. Your friend Randy was right to be scared."

"What do you mean?"

"She looked into that restraining order and found out why it was requested and issued. There is a long list of things that Rachel did to Randy, including breaking into his apartment, keying his car, and puncturing his tires. She was also removed by police officers on two separate occasions from the hospital where he was recovering from his fall off that ladder."

Alex paled as Lana gulped. "Randy's friends were not exaggerating—Rachel did make his life a living nightmare."

"I didn't know about her breaking into his apartment," Alex whispered. "That's freaky."

"I thought you should know. It sure doesn't make his case look any better—if anything, it might give Randy more motive, in the eyes of the Italian police."

Jeremy was right. If they were going to get Randy to the altar on time, they had to find the real killer—and fast.

29

A Simple Gold Band

When Alex knocked on Jake's hotel room door, Lana noticed his fists were flexing open and closed. She took his hand and squeezed, wrapping her fingers through his as they waited for Jake to answer.

When he finally did, Jake had a towel around his waist. He pushed his disheveled hair out of his bleary eyes. "Hey, Alex—great to see you. Come on in, you two."

He stepped back and opened the door further, allowing them inside.

Alex nodded but didn't offer a hand as he walked by Jake. When Lana passed him, she couldn't help but notice how Jake stank like a bottle of whiskey.

Jake blushed as he closed the door behind them, only then seeming to notice his lack of clothing. "I was just about to jump in the shower. Let me pull on a bathrobe. I'll be right back."

Lana hoped he hurried—she could tell by the way Alex was bouncing on his heels that he was growing increasingly agitated.

Seconds later, Jake returned, covered in white terry cloth. "What can I do for you?"

"We know about your prior arrests for assault and that you were following Rachel the night she was killed," Alex growled. "Did you hit or harm her in any way?"

Jake groaned as he sank back against the wall. "What? No! I swear I didn't

142

hurt Rachel. It's true, I had a lot of pent-up anger and a drinking problem when I was younger, but I got help for both and am a changed man."

Lana sniffed loudly. "You sure about that?"

"I haven't punch Craig yet, have I? And he sure deserves it." He turned to Lana, looking at her imploringly. "It's been a tough few days, and I had too much to drink last night. But I didn't hit anyone or anything. I just needed to forget about Rachel and Randy for a few hours, so I went to a bar around the corner and drowned my sorrows. When they were closing up, the owner sold me a bottle to go."

"Why did Rachel's death affect you so badly?" Alex asked.

"I was in love with her and wanted to spend my life with her," Jake cried. He opened the nightstand drawer and pulled out a small box. Lana's eyes widened as she realized what was inside.

Jake opened it, revealing a simple gold band. "I was going to propose to her on the last day of our trip. We didn't know each other long, but it felt so right being with her." He looked up to Alex. "So why would I have hurt her? I wanted to marry her."

"Because she said no," Lana offered. Katherine's assertion that Rachel laughed off her previous boyfriends' proposals went through her mind. Despite claiming to be a changed man, if Rachel had rejected his proposal, he may have hit her in response.

"I never got the chance to ask. I lost sight of her and Randy and gave up. If I had known he was going to the train station, I would have headed there. I figured I would ask Randy at dinner what was going on between him and Rachel, but he never showed."

"Why did you tell her about the wedding?" Alex asked.

"Like I told Lana, I didn't know they knew each other. Randy never mentioned the name of his stalker, and Rachel lied about how she knew him. How could I have known that she was the reason for all this secrecy?"

"I don't care—when Randy invited you, he made quite clear that you were not to tell anyone where the wedding was being held."

"Rachel was my plus one—I didn't think it would be a problem," Jake insisted.

Alex puffed out his chest. "If you hadn't told Rachel, Randy would be at the vineyard with Gloria right now, not stuck in a jail cell. I am uninviting you to the wedding."

Jake mimicked Alex's gesture, locking eyes with him as he moved closer. "Hey, that's not your call to make."

Alex raised an eyebrow at the younger man. "Your anger issues are under control, are they?"

Jake backed down immediately.

"I am going to tell Randy what you did. I don't want to see you anywhere near my brother or his fiancée ever again!" Alex yelled, then stormed out of the room.

Lana started to follow, then turned back to Jake. As angry as Alex was, she understood that Jake hadn't told Rachel about the wedding to be malicious. It sounded like he had seen this trip as a romantic adventure and an excuse to propose to her. This week had not gone as anyone had hoped it would.

"Are you going to be okay?" she asked.

Jake looked so dejected. "Yeah, I guess. Lana, could you tell Randy that I'm sorry?"

The sadness in his voice surprised her. "I will. He'll be sorry to hear you can't make it to his wedding," Lana agreed. *And about your betrayal*, she added in her mind.

When she turned to leave, he cleared his throat. "I know I'm in no position to ask a favor, but would you mind not telling the others about my plans to propose to Rachel? I feel like a fool for thinking she would have said yes."

With one hand on the door, Lana nodded, then exited, wondering whether any man would have been a suitable partner for Rachel.

30

Who Did This?

"Who did this?" Alex raged. He was in quite the funk since their talks with Heather and Jake. Lana shared his pain and frustration. Nobody in their group had a strong motive for killing Rachel.

"It must have been one of them, so someone must be lying about their movements on the night of the murder—but who?"

"Katherine, Bruce, and Craig all have photographs proving they were on the other side of town when the murder happened," Lana replied, knowing there was no point in trying to comfort him. Alex would only find solace in learning the name of Rachel's killer.

"So that leaves Heather and Jake," Alex said.

"Who both deny having spoken to Rachel after she left our hotel," Lana reasoned. As much as Lana distrusted Jake for lying to her and the police, it didn't mean he was Rachel's killer. And though Heather had sabotaged that ladder in the hopes of harming Rachel, Lana couldn't see the young woman viciously drowning her.

"Unless we can find proof that one of them did, it's a moot issue." He dropped into a chair placed next to a small table in their hotel room, then buried his face in his hands. "I can't take this much longer. We can't let Randy down."

Lana sank to her knees and kissed the top of his head. "Don't give up yet, Alex Wright. We'll get your brother to his wedding on time."

"But how?" was the muffled response.

Lana knew they needed to take action, even if it was futile, if only to help Alex cope. She quickly considered their options, settling on the only one she considered viable. "Well, Jake and Heather both claim that they lost sight of Randy and Rachel right before they would have passed the fountain. What if we go back to the Piazza di Trevi and ask the shopkeepers if they remember seeing them that night?"

"The police already did that."

"They only showed Rachel's photo to the shopkeepers, not pictures of Jake or Heather. Maybe someone will recognize one of them or the Straight Up Climbs jackets. It's worth a shot."

Alex considered her words before nodding vigorously. "You're right—those jackets are so loose-fitting that it could be either of them."

"And even if they weren't caught on camera, maybe one of the shopkeepers will remember something that can help us determine which one of them did it."

"Let's do it! In two days, we are supposed to be traveling to Florence for Randy's wedding. I want to see him onboard that train. We have to figure out a way to convince the police that he is innocent."

"And that means finding proof that someone else could have done this," Lana agreed. Talking with the shopkeepers was a long shot, to say the least, but as she saw it, they had no other options.

31

Mischievous Tourists

"So what did Gloria tell you about the video evidence the police found implicating Randy?" Alex asked as he pulled on his windbreaker and headed towards the hotel room door.

"The surveillance footage was grainy, but the Straight Up Climbs jacket made it easy for the police to track him," she replied as they exited and began descending the staircase leading to the lobby.

"They also spotted Rachel following Randy towards the Trevi, but lost sight of both of them right before they would have reached the fountain. They did find footage of her ducking under a hotel's awning when it began to rain. It's the Hotel Roma, one of the boutique hotels around the corner from the Piazza di Trevi."

"That's the little square in front of the fountain, right?"

"It is. The police claim a person wearing a Straight Up jacket grabbed Rachel's arm and pulled her in the direction of the fountain. But the camera was hanging off a café to the left of the hotel, and the rain made it impossible for them to get a good look at the person's face."

"It sounds like we should start there."

"I agree completely. But how do you want to play this? The police must have talked to all of the business owners in that vicinity, if only to find out if they had video surveillance. What can we do that the police haven't already done, other than show them the photos of Jake and Heather?"

"That's already a good start. Plus, I'm not a cop—maybe they will be more willing to talk to me. If I can explain to them, face to face, that it's my brother's life at stake, they might tell us something new that could shed light on who really harmed Rachel."

"It was a windy and wet night; please don't get your hopes up," Lana said, trying to interject rationality into his thought process.

"You mentioned that already. I'll try to temper my expectations," he said before opening the hotel's front door for Lana.

They headed over to the fountain, preferring to speed walk than sightsee. Alex was almost running, he was moving so fast. It took them a few minutes to find the hotel awning the police saw Rachel duck under. Hotel Roma occupied a tiny building sandwiched in between two cafés with large terraces. A short, red carpet marked the entrance, which was covered by a narrow yet deep awning made of diffused glass. Hanging above the door was a security camera, its red light indicating that it was in working order.

When they walked inside, a young man sat behind the reception desk watching the telephone in his hand. He barely looked up when they entered, but did slide a slip of paper and a pen towards them. Lana noticed it was a form to check in.

"Hi, we aren't here to check in to the hotel. We have a question about a friend of ours—a tourist who got into some trouble here two nights ago."

The young man looked up at them sharply. "What kind of trouble?"

Lana pulled out the photos of Rachel, Heather, and Jake that she had downloaded from their respective social media accounts. It was disconcerting to see Jake giving a thumbs up from the top of a rock wall and Heather smiling and waving at the camera. Most disturbing was seeing Rachel striking a pose on a dance floor somewhere in Seattle.

"Did you see any of these people walking by two nights ago at around nine in the evening? There was a storm passing through right about then," Lana added, hoping to prompt his memory.

The man shrugged without even glancing at the photos. "It was raining so badly that night, I couldn't see out of the windows. Anyone could have walked by and I probably wouldn't have noticed them."

148

Lana could feel her mouth drop open. Why wouldn't he look at the photographs? *Does he expect money,* she wondered, *or does he simply not want to get involved?*

She pointed to the entrance of the hotel, hoping to appeal to the man's empathy. "She was assaulted right there under your awning. Are you telling me that someone could have a fight outside your door and you wouldn't notice?"

The young man smiled up at her sheepishly. "Tourists get up to all sorts of mischief, especially when they've been drinking. It's better to stay out of such matters," he said, steadfastly refusing to cast his glance downward at the images spread across his reception desk. "Besides, I'm not chained to this desk. I do have to use the bathroom sometimes or assist guests on the upper floors."

What is wrong with this guy? Lana thought. The receptionist's flippant attitude was making her blood boil.

Alex, too, had apparently reached his breaking point. He picked up Rachel's photo and thrust it into the younger man's face. "The police think my brother assaulted this woman outside of your hotel, but I know he didn't do it! Please help us."

His impassioned plea caused the man's expression to soften. The receptionist took the photograph and examined it closely. "*Bella,*" he whispered.

Suddenly, the door behind the reception desk opened, and an older man strode out. His name tag stated that he was the manager. "What is the meaning of this? Who are you—the police?"

"No, sir," Alex said. "We are trying to find out if anyone working here saw this woman two nights ago." He pointed to Rachel's image. "She was murdered soon after passing through this street, and we hoped someone had more information about the incident. We noticed your video surveillance and hoped you might have caught the assailant on tape."

The man grew pale at the mention of his surveillance system. His eyes locked onto Rachel's photo, her image temporarily transfixing him to the spot. When he recovered, his anger was palpable.

"The police already question me," he snarled in heavily accented English.

149

"Go away—we don't want you here! You leave us alone." He pointed to the door, his expression making clear that he was resolute in his decision.

"Please, sir, my brother's life is at stake! The police think he hurt her, but he did not. And they aren't even looking for another suspect! If you saw anything suspicious, you have to help me. His future depends on it!"

When the hotel manager remained silent yet continued pointing towards the exit, the young receptionist spoke softly to his boss in Italian, clearly trying to reason with the man. But the manager would not budge—Lana and Alex had to go.

"Why won't you help us?" Alex's anguished cry filled the room.

Lana gently pulled her boyfriend towards the door. "Hon, if we get arrested, then there's no one left to help Randy."

That seemed to calm him down enough to get him back outside.

As soon as they were on the street, Alex stared at the hotel's sign. "That guy is acting really suspicious. Why was he so mad that we were asking questions about that night?"

Lana grabbed his hand as a horrible thought entered her brain. "Maybe he hurt Rachel."

Alex took in her words before kissing her on the lips. "Of course! You're a genius. That would explain his intense reaction. Oh no, we mentioned the video surveillance. I hope he doesn't try to delete it. We need to call the police!"

Alex sprinted away from the hotel's entrance and dialed the lead investigator's number. Before the officer could answer, the manager exited the hotel and scurried down the street.

"He's trying to get away!" Lana whispered frantically, pulling on Alex's arm. Just as she began sprinting after the manager, the receptionist opened the hotel door.

"Hey—are you really trying to help your brother?"

Alex stopped and turned to the younger man. "Yes! I feel so helpless—the police aren't even looking for other suspects. But I know he didn't do this. He was at the train station when it happened, but the cops don't seem to care."

The young man nodded in sympathy. "My uncle spent seven years in prison before his lawyer could prove the police arrested the wrong man. It's a horrible fate, being jailed for something you did not do. Your pretty friend was here. Come inside and I'll show you the video."

Lana's heart about skipped a beat as they followed the receptionist back inside and into the office.

As the young man began rewinding the security tapes, he half turned to Lana and Alex. "I was bringing room service to a guest when the fight started, and by the time I returned to my desk, it was over and my boss was walking inside with his girlfriend on his arm. So I didn't see it happen, but he did mention that there were two tourists fighting outside. When the police came by later and asked if we had any recordings of that night, my boss lied and said that the cameras were broken. I knew he was hiding something—they work perfectly. So I took a look at the recording; that's why I recognized your pretty friend."

"I don't understand—why didn't he want the police to see the video?" Lana asked.

"My boss's girlfriend comes to the hotel every Friday, and they stay the night. He tells his wife that he works the night shift once a week to prove to his employees he is dedicated. Ha! My boss, he is afraid if he shows this to the police and they use it to arrest someone, perhaps they will give it to the media and his wife will see him kissing his girlfriend. Here—take a look for yourself."

When he pushed play, he leaned back and let them watch it in silence. The video was quite grainy, its quality made worse by the moonless night and sheets of rain. It was positioned above the door and turned so the camera could see the entire entrance as well as parts of the sidewalk.

The street was empty for the first few seconds, before Rachel ducked under the hotel's awning and shook the rain off her jacket and purse. While she rubbed her hands together, Randy jogged past her, completely oblivious to her presence. His jacket's shiny fabric shimmered in the camera's lens. *No wonder it was easy for the police to follow*, Lana thought.

Rachel froze as he passed, yet once he was out of the frame, she buttoned her jacket back up, then stepped away in his direction. As she did, the hotel manager approached the entrance with his arm around a woman's waist, as they sheltered under a single umbrella. He stopped just before they stepped onto the red carpet and kissed his date, right as another person ran up to Rachel. Unfortunately for Lana and Alex, the person stood directly under the camera, meaning all they could see was a very grainy image of the person's head. *At this resolution, it could be either Heather or Jake,* Lana realized.

There was no audio, but it was obvious from their gestures that this person and Rachel were arguing. When Rachel pushed against the person's chest, the hotel manager noticed the argument and shooed them off his property. Rachel began to run off to the left, but the figure in the Straight Up jacket pulled her to the right, in the direction of the Trevi Fountain.

When Rachel resisted, the person in the Straight Up jacket turned back to yell at her. Lana held her breath as the image of their killer appeared on the screen. Perfectly captured on camera was Jake, and he was livid. When he violently tugged on her arm, dragging her away, Rachel turned back towards the hotel's entrance, her terrified scream caught on camera. The hotel manager and his girlfriend watched them leave, then rushed inside.

Lana could feel a tear running down her cheek. Rachel may have been horrible and manipulative, but she still didn't deserve to die like that.

"Maybe this will help your brother?" the young man said.

"Yes, it will help immensely," Alex whispered. Lana noticed his eyes were welling up, too. "Why didn't your boss call the police when he saw Rachel and Jake fighting? Or try to help her?"

"It is better not to get involved in such things. Tourists can be so unpredictable. Besides, what was he supposed to do—chase after them and risk getting hurt?"

A wave of sadness rolled over Lana. If only the manager had called the police, they may have been able to catch Jake in the act, or perhaps have saved Rachel's life.

32

Tracking A Killer

Much to Alex and Lana's relief, the hotel's receptionist called the police for them, and his description of what they'd seen on the video footage sent four officers racing over.

Alex and Lana watched the policemen as they viewed the surveillance tape, the officers' jaws hardening when Jake was clearly visible in the close-ups. The lead investigator swore in Italian, then turned to Lana and Alex. "Do you know where Jake Segers is now?"

After the police confirmed that he was currently in the lobby bar of their hotel, they rushed back out to their vehicles. Alex tore after them, springing into the back seat without asking.

"What are you doing?" the lead officer growled.

"We are going with you. We can point Jake out to you—it will save time."

The officer mumbled something under his breath, then started his engine. "Close the door," he barked at Lana before speeding off.

Lana pulled the door shut and leaned over to Alex. "I can't believe it. All this time, I thought Jake was so despondent because the woman he loved had died. But in reality it was because he killed her."

Alex nodded tersely, but she could see that his thoughts were elsewhere. Lana was grateful the police were with them; she wasn't certain what Alex would have done to Jake if he'd gotten to him first.

She gazed out the window, watching the city center fly by, wondering whether Jake would try to lie his way out of this. The video hadn't captured him killing Rachel, only pulling her away from the hotel and towards the Trevi. Would that be enough to set Randy free? Maybe not, Lana realized. If Jake claimed that Rachel had gotten loose from his grip and had run off into the night, it would be his word against Randy's, and Lana wasn't certain whose would prevail. They needed Jake to confess, in order to guarantee that Randy would be released.

They had gotten a ride back to the hotel under the assumption that the police would go in first and arrest Jake. However, as soon as the car had stopped, Alex sprinted ahead of the officers, burst into the lobby bar, and made a beeline for Jake, instead.

Lana watched in horror as her boyfriend threw Jake onto the floor before sinking his knees onto the younger man's shoulders. Jake wailed in pain as Alex grabbed his T-shirt and shook him violently.

"We have you on tape. We know you did it! How could you let Randy pay for a crime you committed? You're supposed to be his friend. What kind of monster are you?"

When Alex raised his fist to punch Jake, Lana screamed, "No!"

The officers pulled Alex off of Jake before his fist could fly. It took two officers to hold her boyfriend back.

Lana moved in close to Jake, still lying on the floor. "We saw the surveillance video," she said, raising one hand behind her, in an attempt to stop the police from approaching. She wanted Jake to confess, for Randy's sake. "Did you mean to hurt Rachel or was it an accident?"

"It wasn't supposed to happen like that," he said, his breathing shallow. "She shouldn't have run away from me. It's Rachel's fault that she fell. She slipped; I didn't push her."

"Did you fight about Randy?"

Jake closed his eyes and let his muscles relax. To Lana, it was as if he was giving up. "Yes, we did. I could never figure out why she seemed so interested in Randy, yet never wanted to join our rock-climbing sessions. When I saw her chasing after him, I thought their fight in the hotel lobby might have been a ruse and that they were still a couple."

His face crumpled, and tears began to flow out of the corners of his eyes. "I lost sight of them and was about to give up when the rain started. While I was jogging back, I saw Rachel under that awning and tried to talk to her. When I asked her if she was in love with me or Randy, she laughed at me. She said I was a pleasant distraction but it was Randy she was after. It made me so angry!"

"That must have really hurt, to hear her say that," Lana murmured, hoping he would keep talking loudly enough for the police to hear. All she wanted right now was for Jake to admit that Randy had nothing to do with Rachel's demise, so her friend could go free.

"Why did you take her to the Trevi?" Lana asked.

His face clouded over as the tears halted. "I remembered from our visit that it was under the street level, and I hoped it would give us some privacy. I thought if I showed her the ring, she would forget about Randy. But she didn't even look inside the jewelry box. She tried to squirm out of my grip, screaming about how Randy was getting away. All she cared about was finding out the name of that stupid village. When I wouldn't let go, she clawed at my arms and punched me in the stomach. So I hit her."

A wave of emotion seemed to overcome Jake, and his eyes pinched shut. Out of the corner of her eye, Lana could see the lead officer shuffle closer.

"Did you kill her?"

"No!" he cried. "She started screaming that I had broken her nose and tried to run away from me. I blocked her from getting back up to the street and begged her to calm down so we could talk rationally. I only wanted to persuade her not to press charges. But she wasn't having it—she was going to make me pay."

When Jake fell silent, Lana prompted him again, "And then?"

"I grabbed her arm to try to apologize, but she pulled away and jumped into the fountain and started climbing up the rocks. She had almost made it to the top when she slipped. She hit her head hard on one of the horses' hooves before she fell into the water. I tried to pull her out, but her leg was stuck under one of the rocks. I checked for a pulse but couldn't find one, so I ran away. I didn't want to get in trouble with the cops again."

He looked to the police circling him. "But it's too late for that, isn't it?"

It was chilling to hear Jake tell his story without emotion or remorse. Even now, he maintained that he was not directly responsible for Rachel's death.

"Why did you take her wallet?" Lana asked as two officers approached Jake, handcuffs at the ready.

"To make the police think that it was a pickpocketing gone wrong. She screamed when she fell into the water, and I figured someone must have heard her. So I grabbed her wallet and scrambled over one of the side fences, instead of climbing back up the main stairs."

He must not have been too panicked if he stole her wallet, Lana thought. How much of his story was true and how much was made up for the ears of the police, to cast doubt on his role in her demise?

Lana feared they would never know. She stood up and took two steps back, giving the officers room to move in and arrest him.

33

A Wedding in Tuscany

December 24—Il Pino, Italy

Lana dabbed at her eyes as she squeezed Alex's hand tight. Randy looked so handsome in his tuxedo and Gloria so pretty in her wedding dress. She gazed across the crowded garden, filled with the friends and family of the bride and groom. There was so much love assembled here, it was almost palpable.

Gloria's Italian family had done a wonderful job transforming the vineyard's humble garden into a dream location. Garlands of colorful flowers and lights were strung in between the party tents set up between the many fruit trees. The cloth-covered tables were topped with porcelain plates, crystal glasses, and the biggest bouquets Lana had ever seen as centerpieces.

A gigantic Christmas tree, its branches covered in twinkling lights and a plethora of handmade decorations, stood next to the altar. To one side were several tables filled with more dishes than at an American Thanksgiving. The food smelled so scrumptious, Lana was having trouble concentrating on the extensive vows, given in both English and Italian.

After the priest blessed them and Randy kissed his bride, Lana and the two-hundred-person-strong audience broke out in cheers and applause. The new couple turned to their friends and family, the biggest smiles on their faces, and bowed when the priest introduced them as Randy and Gloria

Rossi-Wright.

Before they could step away from the altar, Gloria's mother set a glass vase wrapped in a cloth onto the ground in front of them, and the Italians in the audience began to cheer. The new couple raised their feet and brought them crashing down onto it, shattering it into hundreds of pieces. Gloria had told Lana that every shard was a year happily married—she hoped it was true in their case.

She felt her eyes watering again as the tension and anxiety of the last few days finally began to dissipate. After all Randy and Gloria had gone through this past year—heck, this past week—they deserved all the happiness a person could want. Now that Rachel was dead and Randy cleared of all charges, she knew they were going to be fine. Gloria was feisty and strong, and loved Randy more than anything. Together, they would be able to overcome any obstacle.

When the band struck up a bridal march and the new couple took to the dance floor, Dotty leaned over to Lana and whispered, "What's with the two last names?"

Lana dabbed her eyes dry and smiled. "Gloria wanted to keep her last name and Randy wanted them to share the same one—in case they ever have kids—so they decided to both use Rossi-Wright."

"Well, I'll be. How modern—good for them. Did you hear that, Earl?" Dotty raised her voice. "The kids are using both of their last names."

"It's a sign of the times, isn't? I like it," he yelled back.

Earl was partially deaf in one ear, but then again, he was also pushing eighty. Despite his age, Earl was an energetic gentleman who treated Dotty like a queen. Lana was glad he was quite fit and didn't seem to be accident-prone. She had enjoyed getting to know him on the train ride to Tuscany; he seemed like a lovely person and a good match for her boss. And Dotty sure did revel in his attention, which was a kick to see.

"What is going to happen to that Jake fellow? Do you think he'll be arrested for murder?" Dotty asked, keeping her voice low.

"That is an excellent question. Jake maintains that he only hit Rachel once and that her death was a result of her fall." Lana paused, wondering what charges would eventually be brought against him. Luckily, that was no longer her problem. The police had Jake in custody, and Randy was right where he should be—dancing with his new wife at his wedding.

When the music died down, Gloria clapped her hands together. "Hey, ladies—it's time to toss the bouquet!"

Squeals of delight permeated the air as half of the party guests rushed towards the new bride. Gloria made a show out of it, teasing the group of shrieking ladies by pretending to throw the bouquet. Her first fake toss took down two elderly ladies huddled in the front. After they had been helped back to their tables, Gloria apparently decided—for the sake of her elders—to just throw the thing.

When she turned around and tossed her wedding bouquet high up in the air, Dotty and three others circled underneath it. Lana's boss elbowed a young cousin to get to it first, twisting her ankle in the process. She landed on the ground with a grunt and cheer, clutching the colorful bouquet in both hands while she looked longingly at her new boyfriend.

"Watch out, Earl, you might be her lucky number seven," Lana teased.

Earl blushed as he held out his hand to Dotty.

"I hope you don't mind me catching the bouquet, Lana. I just can't help myself; my need to catch the thing is almost primal."

"Don't worry—Alex and I are happy living together. There's no need to rush into marriage," Lana laughed, hoping Dotty's remarks wouldn't give her boyfriend any ideas.

"About that," Alex said as he reached into his pocket.

Lana grabbed his arm, her voice stricken with panic. "Don't you dare propose to me, Alex Wright. I'm still getting used to living with you!"

"I'm just teasing. I know better than to push you into any further commitments this year." His eyes twinkled. "I got you a keychain while I was in Portugal."

Lana released his hand, feeling less relieved than she had expected. "Oh."

"It's of a flamenco dancer. I know how much you wanted to go to southern Spain last year, and when I saw it in a shop's window, I thought of you. It's not the same as visiting, but I figured it was better than nothing."

Lana took the small keychain and examined it. The metal figurine was brightly painted in the traditional red and white polka dot dress, and held a fan in one hand and castanets in the other. There was even a lacy fan sticking out of the tiny flamenco dancer's hair.

"It's adorable; thank you!" Lana said and pulled her boyfriend in for a long kiss.

"Isn't that cute?" Dotty said. "That reminds me, Lana, I've scheduled you to lead a trip through Andalucía next Easter."

"That's wonderful. What a great Christmas present, Dotty." Lana released her boyfriend and gave her boss a quick hug.

"We are a couple guides short right now, so you are going to have a busy spring—at least until I can hire a few more with experience. I've got you down for tours in Vienna, Dublin, Oslo, and London before then. Alex, I hope you don't mind Lana being out of town so much."

"Of course not, it's her job," Alex scoffed. "Besides, I can't complain—mine keeps me on the road for half of the year, and I don't see that changing anytime soon. I hope you don't mind, Lana," he said and snuggled closer to her.

"I love you just the way you are, Alex Wright. You don't have to change for me. Our lifestyle might be different than most, but we make it work—that's all that matters."

Alex kissed her cheek. "I do love you, Lana Hansen."

Lana wrapped her arm around her boyfriend's waist and looked out across the garden, filled with laughter and love. *Being surrounded by friends and family really is the best way to spend the holidays*, she thought.

THE END

Follow the further adventures of Lana Hansen in *Death by Leprechaun: A Saint Patrick's Day Murder in Dublin*—Book Six of the Travel Can Be Murder Cozy Mystery Series!

When an old friend is arrested in Dublin for murdering a disgruntled coworker, tour guide Lana Hansen will need the luck of the Irish to clear him of the crime.

Thanks for reading *Death by Fountain*!

Reviews really do help readers decide whether they want to take a chance on a new author. If you enjoyed this story, please consider posting a review on BookBub, Goodreads, or with your favorite retailer.

I appreciate it! Jennifer S. Alderson

Acknowledgments

I want to thank my wonderful family for helping me create the time and space to write, even with the lockdowns and school closures.

My editor, Sadye Scott-Hainchek of The Fussy Librarian, continues to do an excellent job polishing this series, and I am grateful for her excellent work and advice. The cover designer for this series, Elizabeth Mackey, constantly amazes me with her gorgeous and fun designs. Both women are truly a pleasure to work with!

Rome was the first European city I ever visited and continues to hold a special place in my heart. Luckily, my son and husband love visiting it as much as I do! In fact, our last family vacation abroad was to The Eternal City. Like many, we look forward to visiting again soon, once this pandemic is behind us. Stay safe, dear readers. For now, *ciao*!

About the Author

Jennifer S. Alderson was born in San Francisco, raised in Seattle, and currently lives in Amsterdam. After traveling extensively around Asia, Oceania, and Central America, she lived in Darwin, Australia, before settling in the Netherlands.

Jennifer's love of travel, art, and culture inspires her award-winning Zelda Richardson Mystery series, her Travel Can Be Murder Cozy Mysteries, and her standalone stories.

When not writing, she can be found in a museum, biking around Amsterdam, or enjoying a coffee along the canal while planning her next research trip.

For more information about the author and her upcoming novels, please visit Jennifer's website [http://jennifersalderson.com/] or sign up for her newsletter [http://eepurl.com/cWmc29].

Books by Jennifer S. Alderson

Travel Can Be Murder Cozy Mysteries

Death on the Danube: A New Year's Murder in Budapest
Death by Baguette: A Valentine's Day Murder in Paris
Death by Windmill: A Mother's Day Murder in Amsterdam
Death by Bagpipes: A Summer Murder in Edinburgh
Death by Fountain: A Christmas Murder in Rome
Death by Leprechaun: A Saint Patrick's Day Murder in Dublin
Death by Flamenco: An Easter Murder in Seville
Death by Gondola: A Springtime Murder in Venice

Death by Puffin: A Bachelorette Party Murder in Reykjavik

Zelda Richardson Art Mysteries
The Lover's Portrait: An Art Mystery
Rituals of the Dead: An Artifact Mystery
Marked for Revenge: An Art Heist Thriller
The Vermeer Deception: An Art Mystery

Adventures in Backpacking Travel Thrillers
Down and Out in Kathmandu: A Backpacker Mystery
Holiday Gone Wrong: A Short Travel Thriller
Notes of a Naive Traveler: Nepal and Thailand Travelogue

Death by Leprechaun: A Saint Patrick's Day Murder in Dublin

Book Six of the Travel Can Be Murder Cozy Mystery series

When an old friend is arrested in Dublin, tour guide Lana Hansen will need the luck of the Irish to clear him of the crime.

Lana is thrilled her friend Jeremy and his wife are on her tour to Ireland. The couple are having the time of their lives exploring the country's rich literary and cultural history, until they run into Guy Smith, a reporter Jeremy recently exposed as a fraud.

A tussle turns into a fight and leaves each man vowing to destroy the other. Yet cross words and dirty looks tell Lana that Jeremy is not the only client on her tour who has a grudge against the reporter.

When Guy is murdered at the same pub Lana's group is present at, Jeremy is the police's number one suspect. But did he really murder the reporter? Or was it one of her other guests?

Lana keeps their tour going and her ears open for any clues that might help free her friend. Can she discover the true killer's identity before their trip to the Emerald Isle draws to a close?

Available as paperback, large print edition, eBook, and in Kindle Unlimited.

Death by Leprechaun
Chapter One: To Your Health

March 11—Dublin, Ireland

"*Sláinte!*" Wanderlust Tours guide Lana Hansen cried out, mangling the Irish version of "cheers," as she held her pint up high. Three glasses, each as long as her forearm, clinked in the air. Despite the enthusiastic response of her friends, Jeremy and Kitty, Lana could barely hear their hearty replies over the lively Irish music. Everywhere in the pub, patrons were climbing up onto the sturdy wooden chairs and tables to better sing and dance along. In amongst the crowd, Lana could see several members of her tour group clapping and swaying in time with the music, as well.

"I can hardly believe we just flew from the Emerald City to the Emerald Isle," Kitty Tartal yelled over the music before laying her head on her husband's shoulder.

Her words were slightly slurred and her grin goofier than normal. It was understandable; Kitty was working on her second giant pint of cider and was still quite jet-lagged from their flight over from Seattle, Washington.

Lana squeezed Kitty's hand and smiled at Jeremy Tartal. "I'm so glad we get to explore the city together. It's going to be great sharing the experience with you!"

When Jeremy's answer got drowned out by the music, they all laughed and turned their attention back to the band. Randy Wright, Lana's fellow Wanderlust Tours guide, burst through the crowd and plopped down in the chair next to her.

"This is going to be a good group, I think," he shouted into her ear.

Two hours ago, they had welcomed their new group of tourists to Dublin for a weeklong tour. Usually, they started off with a meal in a quiet restaurant so that the guides and guests could get to know each other a little better. Yet before they could finish their "welcome to Ireland" speech, one guest asked whether they could start off by getting a real Guinness, and another seconded the request.

Lana and Randy only had time to introduce themselves before their motley crew was heading back out on the town. Luckily their hotel's location in the heart of the city's center meant they had easy pickings of some of the best pubs in Dublin. A catchy Irish tune wafting out of an open pub door drew them in, and soon they were all drinking and dancing the night away.

"They do seem pretty comfortable here, and with each other, already," Lana replied.

Patrick, a spry eighty-two-year-old, seemed at home sitting at the long bar, where he could easily watch the podium and ensure that his drink wasn't knocked over by an enthusiastic dancer. His flaming red hair and handlebar moustache softened his stern appearance.

His equally redheaded son, Paddy, and daughter-in-law, Nina, were in the center of the tiny room dancing so close that they brought a blush to Lana's cheek. *What an odd couple—opposites really do attract,* she thought. Whereas Paddy had the broad build of a high school quarterback and dressed as if he was a corporate executive, his wife, Nina, was as petite as a ballerina and swathed in a black leather ensemble suitable for a night of clubbing. Most of all, it was the tattoos covering both of Nina's arms that didn't seem to mesh with Paddy's wholesome appearance.

A smile crossed Lana's face when Paddy scooped up his wife and twirled her around, barely missing two pints in the process. No one minded; in fact, the patrons at the surrounding tables cheered them on.

The only person who frowned was Jeanie, a fifty-three-year-old woman traveling by herself. Swaying to the rhythm on the outskirts of the dance floor, she was taking tiny sips of her pint while attempting to dance provocatively. Unfortunately, there wasn't enough room for her intended hip maneuvers, making her dance appear more like she was spinning an invisible hula-hoop around her waist.

On the walk from the hotel to the pub, Jeanie had wrapped her arm around Lana's and enthusiastically told her all about her interest in Irish history, food, and mythology. Lana got the impression that Jeanie chattered nonstop because she was traveling without a companion and was anxious. Her client also did mention that she suffered from terrible motion sickness and that this was her first time abroad in many years, which might be compounding her nervousness.

Dancing a few steps in front of Jeanie was Mitch Anders, a man also traveling without a companion. Lana briefly wondered whether he and Jeanie might be a good match, but something about his laid-back attitude and manner of dressing made her doubt that they would. His skin was so pasty white, Lana wondered whether he was allergic to the sun. He was in his mid-sixties, yet wearing clothes designed for a much younger man. His many necklaces and bracelets jangled as he clapped his hands in perfect rhythm with the musicians. Lana watched his mouth moving and realized he was singing along with the band. *How could he know this folk song?* she wondered, listening for familiar words but not finding any. *He must be passionate about Irish music*, she figured.

Suddenly Lana realized two of her clients were not dancing. She looked around the bar until she spotted Evelyn and Devon Riley in the far corner, well away from the podium. Both seemed nice enough, though quite reserved. The owner of Wanderlust Tours, Dotty Thompson, had asked her and Randy to take extra good care of them and, if they could, to find out why the Rileys had not been touring with her as often as they once had.

Apparently, the couple had not been on a Wanderlust tour in almost a year, which was quite unusual considering they had booked three a year with Dotty's company since it had opened fifteen years earlier. Lana's boss was convinced that they'd had a bad experience on their last trip and were too polite to tell her. When she'd emailed to ask whether they were interested in joining this tour to Dublin, Dotty was so surprised that they said yes that she'd given them a discount as a sign of her appreciation.

Lana leaned back in her chair and observed the couple as she sipped her cider. Evelyn was watching the band, tapping her hand against the table in rhythm with the music. At least, until she noticed her husband was looking at his phone instead of the musicians. Irritation washed over her face as the couple exchanged words, resulting in Devon pocketing his phone and switching his gaze to the small podium. Evelyn grabbed his hand and swung his arm in time with the beat. When she turned to him, he gazed adoringly at his wife. However, as soon as she turned back towards the band, his smile vanished, and he stared up at the ceiling.

What is going on with those two? Lana wondered. Did Devon simply not like Irish folk music? Or were they having marital problems and using this trip to work them out? Lana truly hoped it wasn't the latter, though it wouldn't be the first time a couple had tried that trick during one of her tours. Unfortunately, it usually did not work because the stress of travel amplified the already present cracks and strains in a relationship, instead of offering the couple a chance to escape their troubles.

After the song ended and the explosion of applause died down, Kitty grabbed Lana's hand. "This is the perfect way to begin a week in Dublin!"

Jeremy wrapped an arm around his wife's shoulders and pulled her close. "It really is. Thanks again for getting us these tickets, Lana. We really needed this break."

"Gosh, Jeremy, after all you have done to help me over the years, arranging tickets for this tour was the least I could do. I swear, without your help, my mother would probably still be locked up in a Dutch prison."

"I guess we are even now," he joked.

Jeremy had been her editor when she worked as an investigative reporter for the *Seattle Chronicle*, more than a decade earlier. Over the years, he and Lana had also become good friends, and she had gotten to know his wife, Kitty, and their three children quite well.

She and Jeremy had gone through hell and back after she had been falsely accused of libel and was fired from the newspaper. Unfortunately, because Jeremy was her editor, he also lost his job—something she had always felt personally responsible for. The only bright spot was that he had quickly found another position as editor at the *Snoqualmie Gazette*, a smaller, regional newspaper. What seemed like a step down the career ladder ultimately allowed him more free time, which made it easier to start a family. Now he and Kitty had three beautiful daughters and a lovely home on the outskirts of Seattle's city center.

When Lana had run into trouble during a few of her tours, Jeremy had kindly helped her out by using his connections and resources to discover information she ultimately used to catch a killer, including the evidence that helped free her own mother. That was something she would always be grateful to him for. When he had jokingly asked for her to arrange tickets to a Wanderlust tour as payback, Lana immediately agreed to talk to her boss. Luckily, Dotty was happy to help them out and promised to add him and his wife to the next tour that did not sell out.

"There is so much I want to see and do this week. My co-workers gave me enough suggestions to fill a month in Dublin!"

Jeremy kissed his wife's curly hair. "We'll just have to do as much as we can this week. We should enjoy our seven days of freedom to the fullest," Jeremy said with a laugh.

Jeanie, who had been leaning over to listen in, moved to a chair across from him. "That sounds mysterious. What do you mean, seven days of freedom? Are you fatally ill? Or are you going to prison?"

Jeremy sniggered, and Kitty raised an eyebrow at her. "No," he said. "We haven't been abroad since our girls were born. Being here without them does feel a little like a jailbreak."

"Hey!" When Kitty swatted his chest, he pulled his wife in close and kissed her tenderly.

Jeanie leaned forward and placed her head in between Jeremy and Kitty's, forcing the couple to detach from their embrace. "How old are your girls?"

Kitty took out her phone and brought up a lovely family photo. "Rachel is seven, Rhonda is five, and Olivia just turned two last month."

"They are gorgeous," Jeanie squealed, leaving Lana's ears ringing. "It must be tough leaving those cuties behind for a week. I don't think I could do the same. But then, I don't have kids."

Lana groaned internally at how her tour guest had unintentionally hit on a sensitive topic.

"Yes, well, we haven't taken a vacation in almost a decade, and my parents are fit enough to take care of them all," Jeremy quickly replied in a dismissive tone as a flash of concern washed over Kitty's face.

"The girls are going to be fine," he added as he squeezed her shoulder and shot a glare at Jeanie. "My parents are still in great shape; we have to grab this chance while we can," Jeremy continued when Kitty's somber expression didn't lighten. "And knowing how they like to stuff the girls full of cookies and sweets, our little angels will probably be so high on sugar the whole time, they won't even notice that we are gone."

Kitty laughed. "You do have a great point. I can imagine it's going to be difficult to get them to eat a normal breakfast, instead of ice cream, after we're back."

"That's what grandparents are for," Jeremy agreed. "And we can video chat with them every day. I already taught both my parents how to use FaceTime so we can always reach them."

Lana smiled along, glad to see Jeremy was able to salvage the mood. As much as Kitty wanted to go on vacation, Jeremy said it had taken a lot of sweet-talking to persuade his wife to come on this trip because she didn't want to be away from the girls for an entire week. However, once he convinced her it would be a waste of the plane ticket and their time to fly all the way over to Ireland for a weekend, Kitty eventually agreed. The fact that their weeklong trip was being paid for by Wanderlust Tours made it even easier to say yes.

When the band walked back towards the podium, Lana, Jeremy, Kitty, and Jeanie all turned to view them better. Something unpleasant must have caught Jeremy's eye, because he stiffened up. Lana followed his line of sight, noting that a rather small and overweight man was staring at their table. His sights seemed set on Jeremy, and his expression was anything but pleasant. Someone tapped the stranger's shoulder and motioned him forward. After a moment's hesitation, he narrowed his eyes at Jeremy once more, then walked out of the pub.

Kitty noticed Jeremy's reaction as well. "Who was that?"

Jeremy shook his head, but the puzzled frown remained. "I'm not sure. For a second, I thought I saw Guy."

"No!" Kitty gasped.

"When I told my crew where we were going on vacation, one of the reporters mentioned that Guy had recently moved over to Dublin. My mind must be playing tricks on me."

Kitty cast her eyes downward. "Why didn't you say anything? We didn't have to come to Ireland."

He raised his voice to be heard over the music. "I know you've been wanting to visit Dublin for years and were disappointed that your company didn't fly you over with the rest of the team. When Lana offered us this trip, I didn't know Guy was here. And even if I had, I still would have said yes. We are only going to be here for a few days, and it's one of the busiest weeks of the year, thanks to all the Saint Patrick's Day celebrations. What are the chances of us running into Guy this week? Maybe a million to one?"

* * *

Are you enjoying the book so far? Buy *Death by Leprechaun* now and keep reading! Available as paperback, large print edition, eBook, and in Kindle Unlimited.

Made in United States
Troutdale, OR
09/16/2023

12953239R00100